world's fair, 1992

world's fair, 1992

robert silverberg

FOLLETT PUBLISHING COMPANY
Chicago   New York

Cover by Jack Endewelt

Library of Congress Catalog Card Number: 76-85947

ISBN 0-695-40089-4 Titan
ISBN 0-695-80089-2 Trade

First Printing D

world's fair, 1992

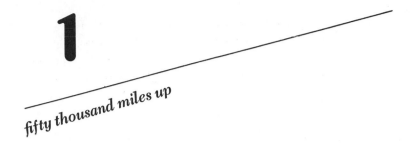

1

fifty thousand miles up

Against the night sky, the nearly completed World's Fair Satellite gleamed like a shiny new penny. You could see it even with low-powered field glasses as it moved in its stately orbit around the Earth: a giant copper-hued globe, the biggest space satellite ever constructed. The Fair's opening day—October 12, 1992—was only some six weeks away. And in very much less time than that, Bill Hastings was going to be up there to begin his year in space.

From every loudspeaker in Denver Spaceport came the booming message: "Attention, passengers for Flight 100, Special Transit to the World's Fair. Boarding has now begun. Please report to Ramp Nine immediately."

"That's it," Bill said. "Here I go!"

He grinned tensely at his parents, his kid brother, and his sister. No one in the family had ever experienced a space blastoff before, not unless you counted ordinary sub-orbital rocket flights to Europe or Asia. He was going to score a Hastings First, and he felt just a little nervous about it. Bill tried to shrug the feeling away. He wasn't going to the Moon, after all, or Mars. He was just making a short hop, only 50,000 miles up.

In a solemn way he kissed his mother, shook his father's hand, hugged his sister, gave his brother a light farewell tap on the point of his shoulder. The rituals of good-bye, timeworn, familiar. His mother had her rituals, too, telling him to be careful, to brush his teeth, to get plenty of sleep. Bill listened tolerantly. Those were the things a mother was supposed to say. His father had very little to say except good luck and good voyage; his sister, who was 22 and getting married at Christmas, was in a general glow of excitement, but not over him; his brother, who was 14, was so frankly envious of Bill's trip that all he could say was, "I wish you could take me along."

He finished his good-byes and turned and sprinted toward the boarding ramp. A power loudspeaker drifting freely in the air above him repeated the announcement: time to board, time to board. All aboard for the World's Fair!

Bill had checked in two hours before. He had turned over his luggage—twenty kilos was what they let you take, same as on a Moon or Mars flight—and they had weighed him. "We won't make any money on you," the weigh-in man at the computer desk had said. Every kilo less of passenger that went aboard meant one kilo more of cargo that could be carried, and so the spaceline preferred to carry lightweights. Bill didn't qualify for that category. At seventeen, he figured he had just about reached his full growth: a shade over six feet tall, a bit under 200 pounds heavy, with a close haircut.

At the top of a boarding ramp stood a trim blonde stewardess carrying the passenger manifest.

"Name, please?" she asked.

"William Hastings."

"Hastings, Hastings, Hast—oh, yes. The contest winner." She pointed to the security scanner. He put his wrist under it, and the place where they had stamped him blazed bright green. They were being very careful about who got up to the Fair before the official opening. Authorized personnel only; there were rumors that threats of sabotage had been made. The 1992 Columbian Exposition was not a universally popular enterprise.

He went through the gate and at last entered the little ship that was to take him into space.

The whole idea of celebrating the 500th anniversary of Columbus' discovery of the New World aboard a space satellite had come into being only two years before—a last-minute brainstorm of the dynamic young financier, Claude Regan—and the special spaceline designed to carry fairgoers into orbit had literally been flung together overnight, as quickly as government safety regs would allow. The ships were double shells of aluminum, with rocket engines generating a few million pounds of thrust. The passengers had to huddle in flimsy hammocklike acceleration cradles instead of the handsome padded couches used now on flights to Mars. These were vessels of a minimum kind, planned for efficiency rather than comfort. Once the Fair opened, they would operate in endless shuttles, continually ferrying people to and from the satellite at fifty dollars a head, with time out only for necessary maintenance checkups.

A stewardess took him to his cradle.

He fumbled foolishly with his straps, and she said, "Is this your first blastoff?" Without waiting for his answer she strapped him in, tugged at the safety to make sure he was tightly secured, and said, "The idea is to relax and pretend you don't have any bones at all. Let the acceleration push you around like jelly. The worst part is over fast."

There were about thirty people aboard the ship. Bill was a little surprised and even disappointed at that; in a funny way it seemed to cheapen his honor to see that so many others were also getting an advance look at the big show. But of course he knew that was silly; thousands of workmen had been up there more than a year, and the place had already been visited by any number of reporters, government officials, design consultants, and others.

A huge man in a sleek metallic suit was ushered down the aisle to the passenger cradle right next to Bill's. He was gigantic in every way, not exactly fat but certainly massive, and he grunted in discomfort as he slung himself with difficulty into a cradle barely big enough to receive him. "This isn't a spaceship, it's a tin can," he muttered in a dark, deep, resonant, instantly recognizable voice. Bill let out an involuntary gasp of surprise. The voice was that of Roger Fancourt, the news commentator who did the eleven o'clock wrapup. And, yes, the face was Fancourt's too, broad and strong, with alert eyes, full lips, dark brown skin. It had never occurred to Bill, in all the years he'd been watching Fancourt, that the famous commentator was so big a man. Even on their new wallscreen, with its life-size image, he had only seen Fancourt's head and shoulders.

It took some adjusting and squirming before Fancourt was properly settled in his cradle. Finally he leaned back and said to Bill. "The spaceline wanted me to pay for two tickets. The network screamed loud enough to be heard on Mars, just to save fifty bucks!" His booming laughter seemed to fill the cabin. "I'm Roger Fancourt. You from one of the news syndicates?"

Overcome with awe, Bill stammered, "N-no, I—that is—it was an essay contest, you see—"

"The high school thing?"

"That's it. I'm Bill Hastings. I won."

"Quite an honor, isn't it? There must have been half a million entries."

"Well, actually, a million and a half," Bill said.

"And the theme—?"

"Life on Other Worlds."

"Right. Slipped my mind." The video man eyed Bill thoughtfully. "Well, is there? Aside from Mars, I mean."

"Your guess is as good as mine."

"You don't mean that," said Fancourt. "Obviously your guess is better than most, or you wouldn't have won. Give me the scoop, Bill."

"What I said was—well, that life probably exists in a lot of places in the Solar System, but not on very many of the planets. So far we know of life on just one world that we've explored—Mars."

"Two," said Fancourt.

"Two?"

"I understand there are living creatures on Earth as well."

Bill chuckled, but he wasn't very amused. "Yes," he said. "But we've been to Mercury, and there's nothing alive there—too close to the sun. And Venus is too hot, too poisonous. Now, we haven't actually made a manned landing on any planet farther out than Mars, but we've sent probes and atmospheric flybys and such, and we have a good idea of what they're like. We know that the atmosphere of Jupiter is a soup of methane and ammonia thousands of miles deep, and that Saturn's not dense enough for anything more than ocean life, if there are oceans there, and the same with Neptune, and that Uranus doesn't look promising either. But in my contest entry I tried to show that we're likely to find living things on many of the bigger moons of the system, like Titan and Ganymede. And also on Pluto."

"Pluto?" Fancourt said. "I thought everybody agrees that Pluto's too cold, too far from the sun."

"That's right. Everybody agrees. That's exactly how I won my prize: by looking at the known scientific facts about Pluto, and working up a theory that seemed to go against those facts, but which actually made a kind of sense. That's what the judges were looking for, I guess. Anybody could toss back to them the latest stuff from Space Authority reports, but to stand the facts on their heads, and to do it convincingly, that's what the judges were after."

Fancourt said, "Can you put your Pluto theory into words of one syllable for the benefit of an unscientific type like me?"

Bill took a deep breath. "It depends mainly on the idea that on a low-temperature world like Pluto—"

A brassy voice said over the ship's audio outlets, "Prepare for blastoff! Prepare for blastoff!" A warning gong began to ring. The ground personnel left the ship. On these flights the budget provided for a crew of just two, pilot and co-pilot. Stewardesses did not remain on board for blastoff. It was too expensive to ferry hired hands back and forth.

Now the ship was sealed. The seconds ticked away. Bill waited, swaying gently in the hammocklike acceleration cradle. He was annoyed to feel beads of sweat forming on his forehead and trickling down into his brows.

The gong cut off. In the command cabin on top of the ship, the pilot was probably transferring control to the navigation computer and settling into his own cradle.

The moment of lift arrived. The ship groaned and lurched as it sprang upward from the launching pad.

Bill went tense and sucked in breath as gravity clawed at him. Five, six, seven G's hit him in a hurry. His face distorted under the strain. Two years ago he'd gone to Japan with his family, and they had taken the polar rocket, but the acceleration there had never gone above three G's. Now it seemed as though a suit of armor, several sizes too small, had been clamped about his body.

But the sensation was only momentary. It was too expensive, and too rough on the passengers, to push the acceleration any higher. The people aboard these World's Fair shuttles wouldn't be trained astronauts. They'd be just folks—though of course they would all need medical certificates testifying that they could stand up to seven-G acceleration. This was one world's fair where the wheelchair brigade would simply have to stay home.

Bill remembered what the stewardess had advised, and tried to go limp instead of fighting the acceleration. Quickly, though, the pull diminished. The engines cut out altogether as the ship reached orbital velocity. Bill had experienced no-grav before, on his sub-orbital trips, but he had never really grown accustomed to the feeling of weightlessness. He more than half expected his liver to come floating up into his throat.

"That's it," Roger Fancourt said briskly. "Now we coast. This your first flight, eh?"

"Is it that obvious?"

"It always is. Feel like telling me some more about your Pluto idea?"

"A little later, maybe," Bill said. "I don't think my brain works so well in no-grav."

They drifted through the darkness. Bill had no porthole to view by—another economy measure—and so all he could do was slump back in the cradle, relax, wait.

Hardly any time at all had elapsed. It was faster to reach a space satellite fifty thousand miles up than it was to drive from New York to Boston. The public relations firm handling promotion for the Fair kept hammering on that theme: just a short, easy hop, skip and jump from your nearest spaceport to the World's Fair. There were millions of people who had never even considered taking a space journey; unless they could be coaxed aboard, the Fair would be a financial flop.

There was still no awareness of motion. And then, briefly, there was: the blast of lateral jets as the ship matched orbits with the Fair Satellite. Bill listened tensely. It was all beginning to seem real to him for the first time— that he, out of all the high school seniors in the nation, had written the prizewinning essay, that he had been awarded a year to work at the Fair before he entered college, that at this moment he was aboard a ship hovering in the void far from Earth.

He felt a second jolt as the starboard jets were fired. This rendezvous maneuver was the most time-consuming part of the whole journey; two objects moving in separate orbits at speeds of thousands of miles an hour had to be brought together in such a way that the airlock of one and the airlock of the other could be joined. A tricky maneuver, but standard in space technique. And, under the circumstances, it was the only possible way of getting Fair visitors inside the Fair. Just as for practical reasons it was impossible to equip passengers aboard short-haul jet airliners with parachutes, so, too, it was unthinkable to provide a spacesuit and the training to use it for everyone who came to the Fair. Professional spacemen could suit up and cross a rope ladder through space to get inside the Fair Satellite, but Earthlubbers would have to move from airlock to airlock without once leaving atmosphere.

Now the ship and the Fair Satellite were joined. The locks hissed open. A new stewardess poked her head inside. "Everybody doing fine?" she called cheerily.

We made it, Bill thought. He plucked at his straps, got out of the cradle, began to move uncertainly through the ship to the airlock. Gigantic Roger Fancourt, just behind him, said, "We have to talk about Pluto some time, don't forget!"

Bill stepped out into the home of the 1992 Columbian Exposition.

It was an awesome sight. He found himself in a high vaulted chamber, brightly lit, walled on three sides and opening onto the airlock on the fourth. In the middle distance he saw workmen welding something, showering sparks about quite casually. Farther away, a giant crane was being inched into position. The bustle of construction work seemed to be everywhere. The shell of the Fair Satellite had been sealed months ago, and the atmosphere generators had been switched on, recycling air through the globe. The entire Satellite turned on its axis, so that centrifugal spin provided artificial gravity, at one G, to keep everybody comfortable. Bill had read how Claude Regan and other promoters had considered pegging the Fair Satellite at half-grav, to make every visitor feel more bouncy and lively, but nothing had come of the notion. A plan to halt the spin entirely every now and then to give everyone aboard a brief no-grav interlude had also been scrapped; it would have been too much trouble to tie down everything portable at such times.

Bill wondered where he was supposed to go. No one was here to meet him, and once he had been checked off the passenger manifest he was left on his own. He hadn't exactly been expecting a brass band, but it surprised him that the sponsors of the contest had left things dangling this way.

After a few minutes he walked over to an official-looking sort and said, "Excuse me, but I'm the winner in the Life on Other Worlds contest, and—"

"The what?"

"The Life on Other Worlds contest. All high school seniors were eligible, and I won, and—"

The man shrugged, "So?"

"I'm here. Where do I go?"

"Better check with the Press Pavilion."

Bill frowned. Then he caught sight of his luggage, coming off the conveyor. He grabbed the suitcase, whirled, and saw that even his not very informative informant had disappeared. Where's the Press Pavilion, Bill wondered?

In the distance he saw the towering figure of Roger Fancourt, and decided to follow him.

It wasn't quite the reception he had anticipated. But at least he was here—fifty thousand miles up, at the first orbiting World's Fair the Solar System had ever known.

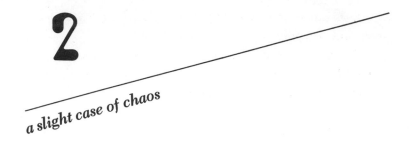

2

a slight case of chaos

Somehow Bill had not expected the Fair to look this chaotic, so close to opening day.

The globular Fair Satellite was divided into many levels for greater floor space, and the pavilions of the nations and the great corporations were rising in every part of the huge orbiter. Workmen shouted across echoing voids; cables trailed everywhere; booms and cranes, which had been assembled out here in space, swung in awesome majesty from one level to another.

There was no sensation of actually being in space. The Earth-normal gravity, the standard atmosphere, the solidity of everything around, gave one the feeling of still being on Earth, and yet not really in any familiar place, for one was definitely inside something, some vast enclosed space.

Bill saw hardly any portholes opening onto the blackness of space outside. Cutting down on the number of portholes reduced the chances of structural weakness in the shell of the Fair Satellite itself, and cut construction costs. All to the good, of course. Still more to the point was the fact that revenue could be produced from the almost total absence of windows.

There were some windows—half a dozen of them, large panels of beryllium glass, widely spaced through the Fair. They were going to be operated as concessions. Anybody who wanted a peek at the starry void—and the promoters hoped that that would be just about everybody who came to the Fair—would have to hand over a half a dollar or so to enter a window area. Penny by penny, the Fair would somehow repay the gigantic investment that had been made in it.

The publicity experts promoting the 1992 Columbian Exposition had seen to it that previous world's fairs had been shown frequently on video: Expo 70, Expo 67, the 1964 New York show, even some ancient movie shots of the 1939 New York and 1933 Chicago fairs. Bill realized now that those fairs and this one had very little in common. The video spectaculars had dwelled heavily on the green meadows, the reflecting pools, the gay fountains, the tree-bordered malls, the gaudy pavilions, all the glittering architectural excitement. Here there were no malls, no trees, no meadows. A single fountain fed water endlessly into a pool, but there was none of the elaborate machinery that had marked the fountains of those other fairs. Nor were the pavilions the Arabian Nights structures of fantasy that had typified earlier expositions.

Everything was simpler, here. Of course. This was a tiny world in space, and anything that was built here had

to be built at mind-staggering expense. It was the Fair
Satellite itself that was the big show here, not its contents.
They had created something new, something the world
had never seen before.

Bill had lost sight of Roger Fancourt, but that hardly
seemed to matter. He wandered on and on, fascinated,
going from level to level, from pavilion to pavilion. Some
of the pavilions appeared to be nearly ready; others looked
as though they wouldn't be able to open for many months.
No one paid any attention to him.

Cornering a workman, Bill asked where the Press Pavilion was, and received rapid-fire instructions: go down
three levels, turn left, take a tunnel past the Atomics Pavilion, cross the footbridge over the thermonuclear display,
go up one level, and make a few more turns and detours.
About the time Bill began to think he was hopelessly lost
he came unexpectedly on a glossy domed building labelled
PRESS.

This was one pavilion that did not look half-finished at
all. Obviously it was one of the first that had gone up,
since publicity was so important to the Fair. It was sleek
and handsome outside and even more elegant within, with
sponge-glass floors, drifting blobs of slave-light in several
harmonious colors, and huge video screens on the wall to
show every phase of the construction work simultaneously.
Trim secretaries in the blue and green costumes of Fair
employees rushed about, carrying stacks of computer tapes
and filing cubes; along the back of the main room was a
computer output rack where journalistic-looking men were
tapping buttons and getting instantly-produced press re-
leases from wall slots; a good many gentlemen of the press
were relaxing in a lounge on a balcony level. Bill saw

Roger Fancourt among them, dominating the group by sheer size.

Feeling confused and out of place, Bill advanced into the center of the room and looked about for some likely office where he could present himself. There was no sign of any. Pretty girls with armloads of documents kept whizzing by, and he had no luck at all in getting anyone to notice him. "Excuse me, miss—" and "Please, miss, I—" and "Could you tell me, miss—" just didn't seem to work in this busy place.

So he had to resort to drastic means to get some attention. Actually, it was just an accident, but it produced the right result. Baffled, annoyed, uncomfortable, Bill decided to go up to the newsmen's lounge and ask Roger Fancourt for help; he turned about suddenly and collided with one of the secretaries, who let out a shriek and went skittering to the floor.

She was a dark-haired girl of about his own age who had been carrying a stack of tape reels so high that she had been holding them down with her chin. The reels erupted from her grasp and went flying all over the room. He helped her to her feet. Her eyes were blazing.

"Idiot!" she snapped. "Why weren't you looking where you were going?"

"I wasn't going anywhere," Bill said mildly. "All I did was turn around. *You* ran into *me*, remember?"

She snorted with fury and began to pick up her scattered reels. Bill knelt beside her to help and said, "As long as you're out of orbit for a minute, maybe I can get a little information from you. I'm looking for the man in charge of the Life on Other Worlds Contest. My name's Bill Hastings, and I'm—" "—the winner!" the girl cried, gasping and letting all the reels she had picked up drop once more. "William Hastings of Denver! What on Earth are you doing here?"

"Well, I thought the Press Pavilion might be a logical place to find somebody who knew—"

"No, I mean what are you doing on the Fair Satellite?"

"It's the prize I won. A year working at the—"

"Yes, yes, silly, but what are you doing here *today?* You aren't supposed to show up until September 10! Mr. Palisander will absolutely foam over!"

She snatched the reels he had collected from his hands and jammed them at another astonished secretary who happened to go by. Then, seizing him by the wrist, she began to pull him across the floor, barely giving him time to grab his suitcase. They headed for the computer wall in the back, then turned left; a section of the floor became a dropshaft as they stepped onto it, and Bill found himself sinking into some hidden level of the pavilion. "I'm Emily Blackman," the girl told him as they descended. "Mr. Palisander's assistant. Look, I'm sorry I called you an idiot, but I did hit the floor pretty hard, and one thing you'd better learn about me in a hurry is that I have a low boiling point. It's my big character flaw." She smiled for the first time.

"Everyone's entitled to one flaw, I guess," Bill conceded. "Mine is a slight tendency not to know what's going on about me. For example, who's Mr. Palisander?"

"Assistant Press Secretary for the Fair. He's the man in charge of the contest you won."

Mr. Palisander turned out to be a suave, dapper little man with close-cropped red hair, a hairline mustache, and eyes of a curious not-quite-olive shade. He did not foam over at all, despite Emily's prediction, at the news that his prizewinner had arrived ahead of time. He listened calmly to Bill's story, asked to see his spaceliner ticket, pursed his lips, and picked up his phone. "Data line," he said. That connected him to the Fair's master computer. Mr. Palisander asked a few questions, nodded, scribbled some notes on a pad. When he looked up finally he said, "You can't ever trust those machines, can you? The more human they make them sound on the telephone, the more mistakes they make. We requisitioned tickets for you for September 10, but the computer must have decided that was too late in the year for you to show. So it sent you tickets for September 3, without bothering to let us know about the change. My apologies, Hastings: we would have been set up better to receive you if we'd known you were coming. Welcome aboard, anyway."

"Glad to be here, sir."

"Have you seen much of the place yet?"

"I took an unofficial tour when I got off the liner. But I don't really know what I saw. I just wandered around."

"We'll give you a better view of things before long. But I suppose the first step is to get you settled. You'll be living in the dormitory on Underlevel Three, and of course you'll be working at the Mars Pavilion, which is on Overlevel Five, and if you'll allow me a moment I'll make all the arrangements." He reached for the phone again. "Emily, give Hastings Press Kit A, will you?"

She took a bulky portfolio from a sliding panel and handed it to him. "This is the orientation kit for first-time visitors," she explained. "It contains a tridim map, an info spread on each pavilion, a list of special events day by day at the Fair, and about a million other things, most of them absolutely useless. You can read it all in your spare time, if you ever get any."

Mr. Palisander put down the phone. "All set," he announced. "Your bunk's ready. Emily, take Hastings over to Underlevel Three and see that he finds the right room."

"But the statistical survey—"

"Can wait."

"We had to arrange computer time a week in advance, Mr. Palisander! And he's got a map, now! He ought to be able to find his own way to—"

"*Emily!*"

"Yes, Mr. Palisander." The dark-haired girl looked sullen again. She glowered at Bill and said, "Let's go, Mr. Prizewinner. I'll show you to your bunk."

Bill had thought more of a fuss would be made over him. Last June, when the contest results had been announced, there had been newspaper interviews, video inserts, a special presentation at the commencement exercises, and more. But now he seemed to be nothing but extra furniture at the World's Fair. He told himself that it didn't matter, really. The important thing was that he was here.

As they rose to the main level, he said "How long have you been working here?"

"Three months," Emily said. "I came up the day after graduation. From high school, that is."

"How'd you get the job?"

"Political influence, same as everybody else. Except you, I guess. I'm the granddaughter of Senator Blackman of Connecticut. This place is absolutely overrun with the grandchildren of big shots."

"I'm not surprised," Bill said. "I applied for a job here

before I had any idea I had won the contest. I got back a form letter saying there was a waiting list of about 150,000 ahead of me, but that I'd be notified if anything opened up. I guess a job here is just about the most desirable in the world, right now."

Emily nodded. "It's going to be a colossal show—if it lasts."

"What does that mean?"

"Nothing much." They were outside the Press Pavilion now. She said, "That ramp leads to the Overlevels, and this one to the Underlevels. There are ten of each. The level we're on is in the middle. The biggest attractions are on Overlevel Five—the Hall of the Worlds and the Mars Pavilion. I don't suppose you were up there while you were roaming around."

"I don't think so."

"You'd know if you had been," she said. "Here. Let me show you how to use your map." She reached into his press kit and pulled out a plastic sphere about the size of his fist. Pointing to a socket alongside the Press Pavilion, she said, "About every hundred yards or so, throughout the Fair, we have a data output. If you want to know where you are, just plug your map into the socket, like this." She released a pair of prongs at the base of the map and slid them into the socket. Instantly the sphere glowed brightly, and Bill saw that a level-by-level three-dimensional representation of the entire Fair was inscribed on and within it. "The red dot," Emily says, "tells you where you are right now. You've got to look close, but you can make out the whole show, ramps and all. Come on, now."

They left the ramp at Underlevel Three and entered a part of the Fair that looked not at all glamorous: row after row of faceless squat buildings, packed together with no effort at graceful design. "Staff quarters," Emily said. "Kitchens. Computer center. Maintenance department. This is the backstage part of the Fair. Not very pretty. They didn't waste any money hiring fancy architects here. This is your dorm."

She indicated a long structure that ran from floor to ceiling of Underlevel Three.

"There's no admittance without a staff plate," she said. "I'll get you in on mine, now, but make sure you get your own first thing, or you'll have problems." As they approached the entrance to the dormitory she turned to face a scanner slot to the left of the door, displaying a polished opal-hued plate the size of a dime that was fastened to her blouse. Bill had taken it for a piece of jewelry, but now he saw it must be some kind of identification badge. It emitted a turquoise glow as the scanner beam struck it, and the door rolled silently open.

"There you go," Emily said. "Tell them who you are and they'll show you your bunk. Maybe I'll see you around again during the Fair—if you're lucky. It's a big place."

"But I—"

The door rolled shut again—with himself on the inside and Emily beyond.

Shrugging, Bill looked around. He found himself in a small drab lobby with a screen in one wall. The screen brightened and the image of a young man appeared. "Mr. Hastings?"

"Yes."

"I'm Conway, the dorm supervisor. If you'll stay right where you are, I'll send one of your roommates down to get you."

A few moments passed. Then a door pivoted open in the rear of the little room, and a plump individual with limp crewcut hair and a disconcerting set of three-tone contact lenses in his eyes sauntered in. He looked to be about twenty. When he spoke, it was as though each word cost him a fee.

"Hastings? Mel Salter. Bunkmate. This way."

He gestured, a languid flip of two fingertips. Bill followed, up a liftshaft to one of the higher levels of the dorm, and into a cramped, windowless room occupied mainly by two double bunks. Discarded clothing lay strewn in mounds all over the floor. The lone table was piled high with music spools, reading tapes, and battered paperback books. A computerized guitar, a pocket piano, and a pair of power ocarinas dangled from hooks on the wall. The wall opposite was completely covered with tri-dim photos of girls, among whom Emily Blackman was instantly conspicuous. The lower berth of the right-hand bunk was occupied by something immensely long and narrow, totally hidden beneath a blanket except for a pair of skinny legs and enormous feet which jutted out to overhang the end of the mattress by half a yard. Mel Salter said, "Nick Antonelli. Sleeps a lot. Guide in the General Chemicals Pavilion."

"Which bunk should I take?" Bill asked.

"Top one here or here. Other lower one's mine. Fourth man gets here October 1. Just dump your gear anywhere."

Finding a clear spot was something of a problem. Gingerly Bill pushed some of the clothes aside and set his suitcase down. Mel Salter settled in the little room's only chair, inserted the earpieces of a headphone set in his ears, switched on a music spool, and closed his eyes. Bill tossed his jacket onto the upper berth above the sleeping Nick Antonelli by way of claiming it. He said to Salter, "Is there some place where I can wash up?"

Lost in his music spool, the plump one made no reply.

Then the sounds of thrashing and stirring came from Nick Antonelli's bunk, and abruptly there loomed above the blanket two incredibly long arms, followed by the head and shoulders and then the rest of what was the tallest human being Bill had ever seen. Yawning, stretching, thumbing sleep from his eyes, he got to his feet in a series of unfolding stages, until at last he stood erect with his head only a few inches below the ceiling.

He seemed to be about eight feet tall, though Bill knew that that was unlikely. Certainly he was at least a seven-footer. He put forth a huge hand in greeting.

"You're the contest winner?"

"That's right. Bill Hastings."

"Nick Antonelli. I hope you don't mind bunking with two slopperoos like us. Do you snore?"

"I don't think so."

"Too bad," Antonelli said. "If you did, you might drown out Mel's. He's got the kind of snore that really gets you—it's a sort of whining thing, like a mosquito coming in for the kill, only the mosquito weighs a hundred pounds. You going to be at the Fair long?"

"The whole year," Bill said. "Working in the Mars Pavilion. Do you know if it's set up yet?"

Antonelli shrugged. "I couldn't say. It's under tight security, and they won't even let Fair employees in until opening day. They've got something in there, that's sure, but I don't know what. You think you can get me in, maybe?"

"First I've got to find out if *I* can get in. And even before that—if you'll show me where I can grab a shower
and spruce up a little—"

"Right over there," Antonelli said. He pointed to a
short dull-colored nozzle jutting from the wall next to the
power ocarinas.

"Where?"

"There. You never saw a molecular bath before?" Antonelli laughed. "This place is run on an economy basis.
They can't afford to import water just to keep mere employees clean. Get your clothes off and I'll show you how
it works."

Bill peeled down. He had heard of these new devices,
but had never actually seen one before. They worked by
sound waves—more accurately, ultrasonic waves—which
bombarded your skin with vibrations pitched to separate
the grime from the skin in one easy process. Stepping over
to the nozzle, Bill watched closely as Nick Antonelli
showed him how to operate the machine. "The marks on
the floor outline the ultrasonic field's sphere of influence.
Go on, step inside the circle there." Bill obeyed. "Now
switch the thing on," Antonelli said. Bill thumbed the on-
button at the base of the nozzle and heard a faint hum-
ming sound. That was all. He felt nothing but as he looked
down he saw his skin becoming visibly pinker and cleaner,
as though he had scrubbed it with a stiff brush.

"Okay," Antonelli said. "That's plenty. How clean do
you want to get, anyway?"

Frowning, Bill said, "I don't feel clean, somehow. I
know I am, but unless I come out dripping wet from a
shower, it doesn't seem right."

"Face up to progress, son. That dripping-wet sensation

is strictly obsolete. Been here long?"

"Couple of hours," Bill said. "I got myself lost, first, and then I found my way to the Press Pavilion, where a not very polite young lady more or less took care of me, although she was very annoyed with me because the computer here had sent me spaceliner tickets for a week too early. That young lady, matter of fact." He pointed to the tridim of Emily Blackman on the wall.

"Dear little Emily?" Antonelli laughed. "You want to be careful with that one. She bites."

"I believe it."

"She's his cousin," Antonelli said, nodding at Mel Salter, who was still plugged in to his music spool and ignoring everything going on. "And her grandfather's Senator Blackman. She sometimes acts like she's Senator Blackman herself. But don't tell her I said so, or she'll shove me through the nearest airlock without a helmet."

"Did Mel get up here on the Senator's recommendation?"

"Oh, no. His father's on the board of directors of Global Factors. Personal friend of Claude Regan himself. Mel's going to be an usher at the Hall of the Worlds."

"And what got you here?"

"A father who's chief executive officer of General Chemicals. Friend, there isn't anybody here who didn't pull rank in some way to get his job."

"Except me," Bill said.

"Except you. Well, we won't hold it against you that you're here on merit. Made any arrangements for dinner yet?"

"I'm not sure what arrangements I can make."

"For one, you can eat in the staff cafeteria," Nick

Antonelli told him. "On the other hand, if you prefer, you can eat in the staff cafeteria. How's that?"

"I always appreciate a wide choice."

"You'll love it here, then." Turning, Antonelli lifted his left foot, extended it across what seemed like two thirds the length of the room, and gently gouged his big toe into Mel Salter's midsection. Salter opened his eyes, blinked, scowled, and took off his headphones. He started to say something, but Antonelli cut him off. "That's enough music for now, Mel. It's time to eat. If nobody reminded you, you'd starve to death in two days."

Salter patted his meaty middle. "Take longer than that. Live off accumulated fat for a month. Like a camel. Hump."

"Humph to you, too," Antonelli said.

They dressed and headed for the cafeteria.

3

to the Mars Pavilion

The cafeteria was a drab metal shed lined with long low benches. At the far end was something looking like a stadium scoreboard on which the day's menu was flashed. As Bill studied it, "Veal Cutlet Cosmique" vanished from the list and was replaced by "Algae Steak Luna Style." Nick Antonelli explained that the Fair's master computer kept an up-to-the-second kitchen inventory; the menu was constantly changing as this or that dish was used up. "The big brain tries to predict the probable consumption of each item on the menu each night, and programs the cooking machines accordingly," Nick said. "But generally it goofs things up, because it hasn't had enough experience with a statistical sample of what we like to eat. By this time of night everything decent is usually gone and the jiffy substitutes start flashing on the board."

"Where do we place our orders?"

"At the keyboard here," Nick said. "Let Mel show you how it's done."

The keyboard looked much like a typewriter, except there was no place to run paper in. Mel studied the menu a moment and began to type. And went on typing for quite a while. As he rattled away, things began emerging from a slot in the wall and gliding toward him: fruit juice, half a grapefruit, a bowl of soup, a salad, rolls, a mound of spaghetti, a quart of milk, and something gnarled and greenish which Bill suspected might be Algae Steak Luna Style. Mel loaded everything onto a tray and announced grandly, "Your turn, comrades."

Nick Antonelli took only a moment to order his dinner: juice and the synthetic steak, no vegetables, no salad, no soup, no extras at all. How he fueled his lengthy body on so little was a mystery to Bill, but at least now he understood why Antonelli was built like an assortment of oversized pipes covered by skin but no flesh. Bill passed up the algae steak in favor of hamburgers which—as far as he could tell—had been made from real meat.

While Bill was midway through his hamburger, which had turned out to be synthetic after all, Emily Blackman appeared and slipped into the seat opposite him.

"Are you organized yet?" she asked pleasantly.

"I'm moved in, anyway."

"Good. I'd like to apologize."

"For what?"

"For the computer's poor taste in assigning you two roommates like Nick and Mel," Emily said, looking at Nick and Mel. Salter went on stolidly eating; Antonelli made a quick face at her.

"They'll do," said Bill.

"Wait till you know them better," she told him.

Bill wasn't sure if he should take her seriously. Before he could decide, she was gone, moving rapidly down the aisle to join a group of girls at the far tables. Nick Antonelli said, "You seem to have made a hit with her."

"Have I?"

"She came over and said hello, didn't she? For Emily, that's quite a step. She's not exactly a sociable girl."

"Not a sociable family," Mel Salter said, between mouthfuls.

"You ought to follow up your advantage," Nick advised. "Get to know her better. Date her a couple of times in off hours, if you can. There's a project for you: the Taming of the Shrew. Who knows? You might end up marrying a Senator's granddaughter."

Bill was so startled he knocked over a glass. *"Marrying?* Who's looking to get married? I won't even be eighteen for another four months!"

"Got to plan ahead," Mel Salter said solemnly.

"Absolutely," said Nick. "It could do wonders for your career, being married to a girl with her family connections. Every door would be open for you automatically. Uh— what sort of line are you going into, anyway? Law? Business?"

"Science," Bill said. "Xenobiological research."

"Xeno—"

"Xenobiological. The study of alien life forms."

"I see," Nick said doubtfully.

"I've already applied for a post on the First Jupiter Expedition," Bill said. "I figure it won't be leaving for eight or nine years, and I'll have my doctorate by then, and I want them to keep me under consideration while they're planning things. Somehow I don't think being married to a Senator's granddaughter would really help me much in that sort of career."

Nick shrugged. "Can't hurt. I really do think you ought to marry the girl, William. The sooner the better."

"Wait a second! I don't even know her!"

"Propose now, find out the details later," Nick said. "Why miss your chance? Right now she likes you, but who can tell how she'll feel about you next month? We could have the wedding ceremony on Opening Day. And then you could take her to Jupiter for your honeymoon."

"Pluto," Mel Salter said. "She's a far-out girl. Needs a far-out planet."

"I'll be best man," Nick volunteered. "Mel can address the invitations. And—"

"Hey, damp it down," Bill said. "I hate to spoil your fun, but I'm just not the marrying type. Not now or ever."

"Ever?" Nick guffawed.

"Well, not for a long while, anyway," Bill said, and invited them to change the subject.

He slept uneasily that night.

There was nothing surprising about that. He was so tired that he barely had the energy to crawl up to his upper berth, an hour after dinner; but it was sheer physical and emotional fatigue, not sleepiness, that gripped him. He had been up nearly all of last night, back on Earth, tossing in excited anticipation of his space trip. And now, what seemed like a million years later, he was actually on the World's Fair Satellite itself, and the excitement of that kept him up again. Through his mind poured a turbulent torrent of images: the spaceport, the journey, the first few moments of bewilderment as he set foot on the Fair Satellite. Colliding with Emily and knocking her tape reels flying. Seeing Nick Antonelli unfold himself to his full giant height. The unfinished pavilions. The ramps and corridors, still strange to him, promising unimaginable wonders.

When he did drift off into sleep it was a sleep punctuated by troubled dreams. He saw himself in space, looking down on the Fair Satellite, which was orbiting faster and faster, spinning so rapidly that its polar antennae were mere blurs, and then suddenly—pop!—it was gone. He saw himself riding in a spaceship, with Roger Fancourt on one side of him and Nick Antonelli on the other; and Fancourt's shoulders were growing wider and wider, and Nick's legs becoming longer and longer, until there was no room at all left in the ship, and the walls began to bulge, and—pop! And then he saw himself trudging across the snowy wastes of a world so distant that the sun was as tiny and as twinkling as a star in the sky, a world which he knew to be Pluto; and beside him a spacesuited figure, faceless at first, who gradually became Emily Blackman, and she was trying to say something to him, but he was unable to hear her, and finally, to catch her words he unfastened the faceplate of his helmet, and—

—pop!

Long before dawn he woke and pressed his face restlessly into his pillow, listening to the high whining sound of Mel Salter's snores. By easy stages the room grew brighter as the artificial morning began. The master computer was merciless, turning up the wallglow exactly as if sunlight were streaming in through a window. There was no sunlight inside this satellite, and not even any window in the room, but no oversleeping among the employees was going to be permitted here.

After breakfast Bill decided it was time he reported to the Mars Pavilion for work.

He went alone, asking instructions of no one. He told himself that if he planned to make his career exploring alien worlds, he should be able to find his way round a single space satellite—especially with a map. Using the map, he quickly discovered, was not all that simple; you had to read it three-dimensionally, which demanded an ability to relate your actual environment to the tiny replica within the sphere. He started off ingloriously by failing to find a ramp going uplevel; it was necessary to retrace his steps, plug in the map, and start all over again, visualizing the spatial layout more carefully. He managed things better this time, and soon was having no difficulties using the map at all. Up to Overlevel Five, turn left, go past the big viewscreen concession, follow the signs to the Hall of the Worlds— that must be it, just past the Global Factors Pavilion—

Bill paused a moment outside that one. Global Factors was Claude Regan's company, and Claude Regan was the man who had created the 1992 World's Fair. Originally, no one had expected the 1992 Columbian Exposition to be held in space. Most big American cities had entered bids for it—New York, Chicago, Boston, New Orleans, Houston, San Francisco, and a dozen others. But the planning commission that was supposed to be organizing the big event hadn't been able to agree on anything more important than the design of its own letterheads, and one day in the summer of 1990 the whole commission had reported itself deadlocked and had resigned. With less than two years to go before the World's Fair, and not even a site chosen.

The President had called in Claude Regan, who at the age of 35 had made himself head of the world's largest corporation. Global Factors had begun as a small finance company; but when catastrophe hit Wall Street, Global was forced to take over half a dozen companies to which it had lent money, and used them as the nucleus for a corporate giant. By 1989, when Claude Regan had gained control of the company, Global Factors had become incredibly wealthy. If it could have declared itself an independent nation, it would have been the fifth most powerful in the world.

A year later Claude Regan had the impossible job of staging the 1992 World's Fair dumped in his lap. It must have taken a lot of persuading to get him to accept, but in the end it had to be clear to him that he couldn't refuse the President's request. Too much depended on putting on a good show. The Fair was important to the prestige of the United States; the country felt that it had to show the newer industrial powers of the world that it still had some vitality and strength left. Nations like Brazil, China, the West African Federation, and Argentina were crowding in on those that had led the world in the middle of the twentieth century. The former leaders—the United States, the Soviet Union, Germany, Japan—were sometimes spoken of as though they were already ancient history, to be classed alongside Egypt, Assyria, and Rome. Here on the occasion of the 500th anniversary of the discovery of the New World, the United States proposed to demonstrate that it was not quite ready to be written off as a fossil.

How could Claude Regan resist such a challenge?

His first act after taking charge of the Fair was to eliminate all the contending cities. Why hold the Fair on Earth at all? Why not in space, that new frontier whose penetration was the twentieth century's greatest's achievement?

In August, 1990, the astonishing plan was revealed: a space satellite 50,000 miles up, with 500 acres of exposition space—making it ten times the size of the largest space station currently in orbit. A whole new line of space shuttles would be constructed to carry Fairgoers at the token price of $50, round trip. The cost of the entire project would be fifty billion dollars.

Construction work began a month later, while Regan got busy raising the money. The satellite would have to be built in space, of course; no booster yet constructed could lift a satellite that large from Earth, and no booster of such capabilities was likely to be devised, since the recoil would be enormous. Girder by girder, the exposition satellite had to be rocketed up to its location piecemeal, and woven together by workmen with shoulder-harness rockets. Unhampered by gravity, they could put the satellite together five or ten times as fast as a similar job could be done on Earth—or so Claude Regan hoped.

And it had been done. Regan got his billions by wheedling, demanding, manipulating, cajoling, and begging, and every day the rockets rose, carrying girders and struts and trusses into orbit. Fifty thousand miles up, a vast and miscellaneous assortment of construction materials had been assembled, spread out over five or six cubic miles and whirling around the Earth as one group. A spy satellite nearby sent telecasts of the work back to Earth. Bill had followed every stage of the work, night after night, as the ribs of the space satellite took shape and as the gleaming skin was laid over them. The shell was finished by the summer of 1991. Construction of the pavilions began that September.

Had anything so magnificent, so fantastic, so wonderfully insane ever been done before in all of human history? A little artificial world in space! What were the Pyramids themselves beside this newest wonder of the world?

Global Factors—meaning Claude Regan—had caused the Fair to come into being. And so it was only fitting, Bill decided, that Global Factors should have indulged itself in this Taj Mahal of a pavilion. Like the Taj, there was nothing gaudy about it; it made its effects through beauty and simplicity, not through dazzling colors or overwhelming size. Perfectly proportioned, rising from a delicate base to widen in the middle, then tapering again to complete the diamond shape symbolic of the corporation, it seemed so precariously balanced that a hard stare would send it toppling. Its marble surface was elegantly banded with a thin line of some darker stone, perhaps onyx. Windows were placed tantalizingly off center in a masterpiece of cunning design. Inside, Bill supposed, there would be exhibits describing all the divisions and subsidiaries of the vast corporation, and that did not sound at all exciting, but the outside of the building could atone for a great deal of commercial dreariness within.

Just beyond the Global Factors pavilion lay the Hall of the Worlds. It rose two levels high, with a colossal copper-covered double door standing slightly ajar and beckoning him within. There seemed to be no reason why he could not go inside, and so he strode up the stone walkway that led to the door and entered.

He found himself in a realm of blackness—and eerie silence.

The silence was overwhelming, almost painful. The Hall of the Worlds was so quiet that he could hear the thunder of his own blood coursing through his body, a faroff drumbeat. Bill realized that the place must be a giant anechoic chamber, soundproofed to kill even the slightest echo or reverberation. The purpose, undoubtedly, was to create awe—and it succeeded.

As his eyes grew accustomed to the darkness, he saw the worlds themselves, moving slowly along their orbits. The hall was designed as a miniature replica of the Solar System; but one vital component seemed to be out of commission, for only the feeblest of glows came from the sun, high overhead in the center of everything. By that dim beam Bill was able to pick out little Mercury, whirling along at a good pace, and Venus and the Earth. Mars seemed missing, but he found it on the far side of the sun, in opposition to Earth. Great Jupiter and ringed Saturn swept serenely along; Uranus and Neptune scarcely appeared to be moving at all; and Pluto, Bill's own special world, was a faint sphere at the rim of the hall, seemingly frozen in its track.

Whatever mechanism moved the planetary models was invisible, and so, too, were the connecting rods; each of the worlds appeared to drift freely in space. The models had been prepared carefully, according to the latest research, and showed every geographical detail with fine clarity. Mars was properly pockmarked with craters; Jupiter seemed swathed in thick mist; Saturn's rings appeared to be composed of thousands of tiny pebbles miraculously held in the same plane. In this dark and silent place Bill felt himself elevated almost to a godlike stature. It was not hard to imagine that he floated in the void with all the heavens laid out about him for his inspection. A chill of wonder slithered down his back as he stared across billions of miles to icy Pluto.

A voice said, flat and dead in the anechoic room, "Okay, Joe, grab that rheostat and give the sun some juice!"

That raucous shout was like a desecration. Bill stood stunned at the breaking of the mood. The model of the sun brightened; the room, though still dark, now was more clearly illuminated, so that the whirling clusters of moons about the two big planets came into view, and night and day were plainly marked on each world, and as he watched Earth's moon it was engulfed by shadow and vanished into brief eclipse. Now Bill became aware of balconies from which spectators would watch the show, and he saw workmen stringing loops of cable, adjusting the sound-proofing panels, and clocking the movements of the heavenly bodies. He became aware of a stocky figure that had appeared beside him: Mel Salter.

"Good show?" Mel asked.

"Marvelous."

"Lucky thing you weren't here to see it last Tuesday. The computer got a little sloppy. Sent Venus moving the wrong way on its orbit. Then Neptune lost a moon and Jupiter and Saturn crossed orbits and almost collided. Pretty wild. Technicians screaming all over the place."

"Is it likely to do stuff like that after the Fair starts?"

"Anything's likely," Mel said. "Looks right nice today, though. Eh?"

"It's very impressive. What will the show be like?"

"Audience files in up there. Music coming from a thousand little speakers floating near the ceiling. Man with deep voice tells them of mystery and wonder of Solar System. We show a couple of eclipses, bring a comet through, and so on." Mel grinned. "Planetarium stuff. What's important is the feeling you get, being out in space. End of show, we open door in back, feed the crowd on into the Mars Pavilion."

"Out that door?"

Mel nodded. "Not yet, though. Nobody's getting into the Mars Pavilion who doesn't belong. I've tried."

"*I* belong there," Bill said. "Come on with me. Maybe we can both get inside right now."

Mel Salter shook his head. "Be lucky if you can get yourself in. I'll stay here. I'm supposed to be working, anyway."

Bill went on alone through the door at the back of the Hall of the Worlds, passing under Pluto as he stepped out. Behind him he could hear Mel Salter shouting instructions to one of the workmen; here, at least, Mel seemed to escape from the sluggishness that gripped him elsewhere.

The door led him into a narrow corridor whose walls were painted with murals depicting the constellations. An electrician was rigging what probably were black light projectors near the ceiling; he looked down at Bill and called, "Hey, where you going?"

"Mars Pavilion."

"Closed. Authorized personnel only."

"It's okay," Bill said. "I work there."

He kept going, following the corridor through several twists and turns, and came eventually to a crude and obviously temporary barrier of thick wooden planks that completely blocked the path. There was a hand-lettered sign that declared:

NO ADMISSION
ENTRY FORBIDDEN BEYOND THIS POINT

Bill saw no way to announce his presence. He hunted in vain for a bell, a knocker, a scanner outlet. Puzzled, he hammered on the door with his fist, but got no answer. Looking up, he saw what he thought might be the eye of a security monitor in the ceiling, and—feeling faintly foolish—said to it, "Will you let me in? I'm Bill Hastings. The essay contest winner."

Nothing happened.

Ten minutes later he was still standing outside the Mars Pavilion, wondering what to do.

Bill began to think he should have tried to phone some Mars Pavilion official from the dorm to say that he had arrived—perhaps Dr. Martinson, the xenobiologist in charge of the Old Martians—instead of just coming up here on his own. But he hadn't realized that things would be so closed up.

Then what had seemed to be a solid section of the corridor wall pivoted open abruptly and Bill found himself confronted by a short, thin, stern-looking man dressed in shabby, stained work clothes. His white hair was long and unkempt; his pale blue eyes were fiercely inquisitive. He looked like a gardener or a handyman of some sort.

"Well?" he snapped. "What are you standing here for?"

"I—I'm—I'd like to get into the Mars Pavilion."

"Nobody gets in until Opening Day! That's the rule here! Dr. Martinson's orders!"

"I know," Bill said. "But I'm supposed to be working

for Dr. Martinson in the Pavilion. I just arrived yesterday, and—"

"What's your name?"

"Hastings. William Hastings."

"Wait here," the little man commanded. "Don't go anywhere!"

As mysteriously as he had appeared, he disappeared back into the wall. The swinging block closed again, sealing so smoothly that Bill searched in vain for the join.

Five more minutes went by. Bill was getting annoyed, now. He didn't like being shouted at by a handyman, and he particularly disliked being left standing around all the time as if he were somebody's unclaimed baggage.

The wall opened once more. The little handyman returned, looking angrier and more fierce than ever.

He said severely, "I've checked! William Hastings is not due to arrive for six more days!"

"That's right, but the computer made a mistake, and—"

"All right. I know. You're here, and that's that. I suppose we'll have to let you in, Hastings. Follow me." He stepped through the opening in the wall. Bill followed. The small man put his palm to a scanner plate on the inside wall and the swinging section shut. Bill found himself in what looked like an airlock, stuffy and poorly lit. His guide touched his thumb to a second scanner plate on the inner wall, and, as the airlock door slid open, looked over his shoulder and smiled for the first time. "My name's Martinson, young man. Welcome to our show."

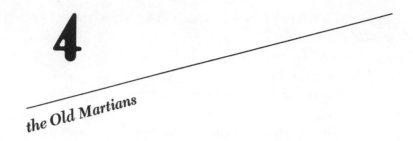

4

the Old Martians

The Mars Pavilion seemed to consist of nothing but rooms within rooms. The outer airlock led to a second chamber, narrow and curving away in both directions; blowups of tridim photos of the surface of Mars were mounted on the walls, but Bill got only a glimpse of them before Dr. Martinson beckoned him through another sliding panel into a third room of the same shape that housed other exhibits, and then instantly on to a fourth. Bill guessed that the pavilion must be circular, with each of these chambers going completely around the whole structure, but everything was so dark that he could form no clear idea of the layout.

The fourth room was bare except for a gleaming metal door along its inner surface. Dr. Martinson said, "The Old Martians live behind there." He put his thumb to the scanner plate, and the door began slowly to open.

Bill wasn't sure which was more exciting—to be reaching the core of the Mars Pavilion or to be standing next to Dr. Lionel Martinson of Columbia University, the world's ranking authority on xenobiological problems and one of his own personal heroes. He wondered if he could ever bring himself to admit to Dr. Martinson that he had mistaken him for a handyman. Of course, he had never seen the famed scientist in person before, and even tridims could be misleading; in his pictures Dr. Martinson's hair was combed, he wore eyeglasses and a business suit, and his expression was usually relaxed and pleasant. Bill hadn't associated the professorial man in those pictures with the rumpled, haggard, disreputable-looking person who had emerged from that sliding wall-panel.

"There's only one person in this whole World's Fair," Dr. Martinson said, "who can open these doors with his own fingerprints alone. That's myself. Everyone else who's authorized to get into the Mars Pavilion—and there aren't many of those—needs to have some other authorized person with him to get in. Combinations of prints are necessary. That is, the scanner will accept your prints, say, in combination with those of two other authorized individuals, and will open up. But if you come in alone, or with just one other member of the pavilion staff, you won't get through. Most of the people here need three-way combinations to get the doors open. A few are programmed two-way. You'll be programmed three-way. And now, I think, we can go ahead."

They stepped into the innermost chamber.

Bill saw nothing. The room was completely dark.

"Of course," Dr. Martinson went on, "you understand

that we have to take all precautions. If anything went wrong with the pressurization or atmosphere of the dwelling chamber, the inhabitants would die in a hurry. So we have a fail-safe system here of four airtight chambers surrounding the dwelling chamber itself. The airlock hatches are programmed so that no more than one can be open at any time."

The door slid closed behind them. As it did, the lights came on, and Bill gasped at what he saw. The Hall of the Worlds, with its models of the planets, had been designed to give an illusion of otherworldliness, but it hadn't seemed like anything more than clever make-believe to Bill. This was very different. It was like stepping through a magic doorway and arriving on Mars.

Behind a thick ceiling-high pane of protective glass was what appeared to be a Martian cave. One main room was visible, and several smaller chambers branching off. Each room was furnished simply, with little beds of plant fibers placed Japanese-fashion on the floor. Some of the rooms were decorated with wall paintings that looked a million years old, the paint pale and dim, the designs abstract and mysterious. The only illumination in the cave came from the broad leaves of a grayish plant; a pot of it sat in a corner of each room and gave off a faint yellow glow.

Quietly going about their business behind the glass wall were six gnomish beings, hardly more than three feet high, with dry, leathery gray skins and fragile, pipestem-thin arms and legs. Their heads, large and bald and spherical, seemed to be on the brink of toppling right off their flimsy necks. Two enormous eyes, a tiny nose, and a slit of a mouth comprised the features of the Old Martians.

Occasionally they glanced toward the pane of glass. But they did not indicate any sign of awareness of their two observers.

"It's one-way glass, of course," Dr. Martinson said. "They think they have privacy."

Bill nodded without replying. He was totally absorbed by the sight of the alien creatures before him.

He couldn't count the number of times he had watched the documentaries on the discovery of the Old Martians— the biggest single event thus far in man's conquest of the Solar System. The first explorers to reach Mars—a Soviet team, in the 1970's—had thought that the red planet was nearly as dead as the Moon. The deserts were endless stretches of bleak sand, pockmarked by the craters of meteor collisions. There was no water anywhere, and the atmosphere was the next thing to vacuum. A few rocks studded the emptiness, sturdy boulders of incredibly brilliant colors, blues and reds and greens. The only life-forms in sight were the splotches of grayish-green vegetation that stained the red sand.

But the second manned expedition to Mars, sent up by the United States a year later, had the honor of discovering that there once had been a civilization there. Networks of underground caves held alien skeletons, artifacts, enough material to create a new branch of archaeology overnight. Carbon-14 datings revealed that the caves had not been inhabited for more than ten thousand years. Scientists assumed that the Old Martians had become extinct long before Egypt's first pyramids had been erected.

The sensation over the Old Martians gradually died down as the New Martians—the colonists from Earth—began to take possession of the planet. The first settlers were the Russians, who built a small dome-covered outpost in the Aurorae Sinus region, just north of the Martian Equator. It was a miniature imitation of Luna City, the United Nations-sponsored dome on the Moon, but because of the general economic troubles in the Communist world in the 1980's it never amounted to much.

A second dome was put up in 1983—Marsport, the first real city on Mars. A group of private firms from the United States and Europe had put up the capital to found Marsport, and thousands of volunteers headed for the new frontier in space. A few years later a third dome was established as a joint project of China, Brazil, and Nigeria. Mars, under its Earthborn settlers, boomed as it had never boomed before.

And in 1989 a prospector scouting the desert a hundred miles from Marsport stumbled into a cave looking for precious metals, and found living Old Martians instead.

If the discovery of their remains had caused a sensation, the news that the Old Martians had survived into the twentieth century created global pandemonium. The story occupied the front pages for months. There had never been a scientific event to match it for popular interest—it far outdid the finding of Tut-ankh-amen's tomb, the explosion of the first atomic bomb, the launching of the first space satellite, and the first manned landings on the Moon and Mars.

The first cave had contained about a hundred of the Old Martians. Other caves had been discovered later, and it was thought that the total Old Martian population was no more than about ten thousand. Most of them kept well out of sight, never venturing to the inhospitable surface of their world.

Archaeologists believed that at the best times the Old Martians had never numbered more than a few million; Mars simply was unable to support many people unless, like the dwellers in Marsport and the other domes, they had full control over their own environment and were able to manufacture synthetic foods. Somehow—no one yet knew why—the birthrate of the Old Martians had begun to drop off thousands of years ago; each year there were fewer of them than the year before, and at their present rate of decline they would probably be gone altogether in another three or four centuries. They gave the appearance of being a dying race: small, delicate, weary of the universe, waiting for the end to come.

Bill had been fifteen when the news of the Old Martians' discovery broke. Then and there he knew what his career was going to be—to go out to the worlds of space, to investigate the creatures that might live on them, to study the different forms life takes on different planets. At the moment, the Old Martians were the only alien life-form ever discovered, except for the Martian plants and a few Venusian viruses; but there was plenty of the Solar System that man was yet to visit.

Dr. Martinson said, "Would you like to go into the cave?"

Startled, Bill blurted, "Can we?"

"If they don't object. I'll ask them."

He opened a small panel in the side wall, revealing a metal grille. "This is Dr. Martinson speaking," he said. "May we enter your dwelling?"

One of the gnomes peered toward the glass wall and replied—in a high-pitched, flutelike voice and in unmistakable English—"If you wish."

"They speak English?" Bill asked, astonished.

"A few of them do. Most of them aren't interested in learning."

"And do we understand their language?"

"A dozen words or so," Dr. Martinson said. "Learning more is one of the projects we hope to accomplish during the Fair. They aren't terribly interested in teaching us. I'd say that in general they aren't terribly interested in us at all. They just tolerate us, more or less. Mostly less. So we record everything they say, and feed it to our computer for analysis, and hope to figure out their speech patterns without their help. Come this way."

He led Bill through another of the unexpected swinging panels that seemed to be hidden all over the Mars Pavilion, and into a tiny room adjoining the vestibule of the dwelling chamber. From a collapsible closet Dr. Martinson drew what looked like two yellow raincoats and a pair of breathing masks.

"Thermal suit," he said, handing one of the "raincoats" to Bill. "It's cold in there. We never let the temperature rise more than two or three degrees above the freezing point. And you'll need the mask, too."

"I thought it was possible for Earthmen to breathe the atmosphere the Old Martians use."

"It is. It's an oxygen-nitrogen mixture, but the proportions are a little different, higher on the nitro, lower on the oxy. And we keep the pressure low. So you can breathe it, but it's pretty thin stuff—something like the air on top of the Himalayas or the Andes. You'll be much more comfortable with the mask."

When they were properly equipped, the xenobiologist opened still another airlock, which gave them access to a short angling corridor that ended in one of the familiar metal doors. Bill wondered how long it had taken to design the maze of interior chambers that made up the Mars Pavilion. The way things were set up, the public and the scientific staff each had access to the Old Martians, but there was little or no chance of an accidental contamination of the dwelling chamber's atmosphere by the heavier, richer air breathed by Earthmen. Although Earthmen could tolerate the atmosphere of a Martian cave without serious harm, it did not work the other way, Bill knew: a few minutes of breathing Earthlike atmosphere would be fatal to the little beings.

Both airlocks were shut. Pumps throbbed; the air went whistling out, and the thin Martian atmosphere filtered in. The inner door opened. Dr. Martinson stepped forward, and Bill followed him into the dwelling chamber.

The six Martians took little notice. Two appeared to be asleep; a third sat crosslegged on a fiber mat, in what seemed to be deep meditation, even a trance; another was weaving a new mat, and the last two stood near the wall of glass, doing nothing in particular. Dr. Martinson approached the one who was weaving and said something in a clicking, harsh language that sounded like the scraping of insect wings. The Martian looked up slowly and replied in English, "Stay as long as you wish."

Dr. Martinson said, "This is William. He will be working here with you."

The Martian did not reply. He eyed Bill briefly and went back to his weaving.

"What were you saying to him?" Bill asked.

"It's a phrase of greetings, a way of expressing thanks for being allowed in here. It's practically the only Martian sentence that we think we speak correctly. You'll have to say it every time you come in here. Try repeating it after me." He uttered the scraping sounds again.

Bill did his best to imitate them. His best wasn't very good. But Dr. Martinson merely looked amused. There was actually a twinkle in his forbidding blue eyes. "Try again," he said, and spoke the phrase.

Bill tried again, not very much more successfully.

"It takes practice," said the xenobiologist. "Don't worry about it. Look here, now. You know where the Old Martians get their air and water? Yes, of course you must know. You've studied all this already, haven't you?"

"I've tried to keep up with your reports, yes."

"Don't be modest, Hastings! I read your essay. Quite fine work! Of course, your ideas about Pluto are somewhat radical, but all the same, you've clearly given careful thought to xenobiological problems. Quite fine work! Look —these are the oxygen-emitters."

He indicated stubby whitish plants with thick drooping leaves. On Mars they grew in every inhabited cave, manufacturing enough oxygen to meet the Old Martians' needs. They were, Bill knew, a major scientific puzzle. Earthly plants also manufacture oxygen as a byproduct of the process of photosynthesis, by which they convert carbon dioxide to starch for food. But photosynthesis takes place only in sunlight and with the aid of the green substance known as chlorophyll. These Martian plants lived underground, receiving only dim artificial illumination, and had no chlorophyll at all. How did they produce oxygen, then? No one knew, except perhaps the Old Martians, and they weren't telling.

In a different chamber of the cave were three stone

pots containing another kind of plant. From a thick central stem grew a number of dangling ropelike shoots, at the end of each of which sprouted a swollen maroon pod about the size of a child's fist. Dr. Martinson glanced at one of the Martians, who as if on cue picked up one of the stems and pinched the pod from its end. A few droplets of water ran out. The Martian put the pod to his thin-lipped mouth and squeezed it, taking a deep drink.

"On Mars, as you probably know," said Dr. Martinson, "the roots of the water plants go down hundreds of meters. They tap underground pools and springs that were formed millions of years ago, when Mars still had surface water. Here we've had to install water tanks beneath the dwelling chamber."

"And the Martians drink the same water we do? What about the minerals and other impurities they're accustomed to?"

"A good point. We have medical opinions that the Martians could probably get along on the same H_2O that the Fair uses. But just to be safe, we've lined the water tanks and conduit with soil and rock excavated from an actual Martian site. The water we feed in is standard, but it has some time to pick up residual impurities before the Martians drink it. So far they haven't complained. Want a taste?"

"If nobody minds," Bill said.

Dr. Martinson asked permission of one of the Martians and snipped a second pod from the plant. Bill put it to his lips. The water was cool and faintly tingly, as though it had been carbonated; the flavor was excellent.

He followed the scientist through the little chambers of the cave. They contained nothing but the fiber mats and

57

pots of various types of plants to provide oxygen, water, and food; there was no furniture, and Bill saw no personal possessions and only a few simple tools. The Martians claimed to have a rich literature of history and poetry, but nothing that might be considered a book was in view. From what little was known of Old Martian literature, it seemed to be entirely unwritten, carried in memory from generation to generation. Bill was aware that scientists on Mars were attempting to record some of this literature while there still were Old Martians alive who remembered it, but evidently not much had been achieved along those lines yet, because of language barriers and the unwillingness of the alien beings to offer more than token cooperation. They just did not care whether their works lived after them, it appeared.

Bill said, "Is this an actual Martian cave, or an imitation constructed here?"

"An actual cave," Dr. Martinson told him. "We had it ripped up slab by slab and reassembled on the Fair Satellite. The soil you see here, the stone pots, everything—all of it genuinely Martian."

"That must have cost a fortune!"

"I suppose it did. But it was necessary. We had to be absolutely certain that the Martians would feel at home in this transplanted environment. There aren't so many of them left that we can take chances with the health even of a few."

"I'm surprised that the government was willing to risk letting them be brought here at all."

"That's a long story," Dr. Martinson said, and for an instant his eyes flashed with the same fierceness he had displayed outside the pavilion. "Let's not discuss that now.

It's time to leave, anyway. We mustn't abuse their hospitality."

Bill was unwilling to leave. He had spent no more than ten minutes in the dwelling chamber, but already he had begun to feel that he was on Mars, and he resented being pulled away from these fragile, fascinating beings. Withdrawn and passive though they were, they had to be admired for their sheer ability to survive. Long after the collapse of the Martian civilization, these few remnants still clung to their caves, going through the motions of existence, living out the final days of their species. They were completely self-sufficient, never needing to leave their caves at all; but they lived right at the margin of possibility, having exactly what they required for survival and nothing more. Any expansion of their numbers and they would die of starvation and thirst.

These people, Bill thought, are the opposite of Earthmen. Here we are bursting forth from our own planet, colonizing the Moon and Mars, probing Venus and Mercury, thinking about exploring the outer planets, spilling all over the Solar System. And here *they* are, huddling in caves, tired, quiet, resigned. We're so very young. And they're so terribly ancient.

"This way," Dr. Martinson called.

They did not leave the dwelling chamber by the airlock they had used to enter it. What looked like a flat, rough rock in one of the smaller rooms was really a trapdoor; Dr. Martinson pulled it up, and he and Bill descended into a self-contained cubicle beneath the floor of the dwelling chamber. The ritual of replacing the Martian atmosphere with one fit for Earthmen took only a minute; then they left the airlock at its lower end and descended on a winding metal staircase into a large, brightly lit room on the level below. They had reached the basement of the Mars Pavilion. Half a dozen people in laboratory smocks were there, all of them busy: one bent over a microscope, one typing something on a computer's input keyboard, one listening to a recording on earphones and scribbling notes, another checking a row of dials and meters, one arguing bitterly on the telephone, and the last, a woman with close-cropped red hair, studying a video screen that re-layed views of the Old Martians in their chamber above.

"Our scientific staff," Dr. Martinson said. "I'll leave you to make your own introductions when you have the chance. While you're with us, you'll consider yourself to be the general assistant to the entire staff, and will carry out any assignment that anyone in this room gives you. Is that quite clear?"

"Yes, sir."

"Good. If there are any problems, let me know." He vanished into an adjoining office.

Once again Bill had been left on his own, and once again he stood by, feeling out of place and adrift, waiting for someone to see him. What might have been several years later, the man who had been on the telephone slammed it down in rage, glared at it as though he wanted to throw it through the wall, and, making a visible effort to control his temper, got up and came over to Bill.

Bill said, "I'm Wil—"

"I know. I saw you on the screen when Doc brought you in. I'm Lou Pomerantz. Glad to know you, Hastings."

He shook hands with Bill in a tense, impatient way, as though shaking hands were too trivial an operation to devote much time to. Pomerantz was short and stocky, with dark wavy hair, thick eyebrows that merged above the bridge of his nose, and a taut, rigid expression. He was about thirty, Bill guessed—a graduate student in xenobiology, most likely, a year or two away from his doctorate.

"Morons," Pomerantz muttered. "Apes!"

"Who?"

"The Press Pavilion people. Every day, without fail, they call up and try to get permission to send a bunch of reporters through here. Every day! And when I scream and rant at them, they simply say that they thought perhaps we've changed our mind. I'd like to get my hands on that Palisander character, or his snippy little assistant Miss Blackman, and—"

"But why *is* the Mars Pavilion closed to the press?" Bill asked. "It seems to be all finished, and the Fair opens in five weeks, so—"

"It's a long story," Pomerantz sighed.

Dr. Martinson had used the same phrase in another context. Bill wondered if he was ever going to hear that long story. But he had no chance to ask, for the restless, harried Pomerantz already had him by the elbow and was propelling him around the laboratory. The dials and meters, he was saying, monitored the environment in the dwelling chamber, reporting on air pressure, atmosphere content, humidity, and temperature. "We watch those dials round the clock in three-hour shifts," Pomerantz said. "Of course, the master computer is supposed to keep watch and notify us if the environment slips off the programmed parameters in any way, but who trusts that crazy computer? *We* don't. We sit and stare at the dials, and we move fast if anything looks like it might be going wrong.

Now that you're here, we've all got that much less staring time to put in. We'll have you in the rotation by tonight. Now, over here, Dr. Milbank is playing back a recording of Martian conversation and trying to make sense of it by checking it against a computer analysis. Dr. Chiang is making a microscopic examination of a stem section from an oxygen plant. That's Sid Webster, watching the environment monitors. Nate Kuharich is giving the computer the raw data on the psychological experiments that Dr. Sullivan is conducting. Dr. Sullivan is checking on one of her experiments now."

Bill tried to match names to faces, but the information had been thrown at him too quickly to absorb. He wouldn't have any trouble remembering which member of the team was Dr. Chiang, and Dr. Sullivan was the redheaded woman watching the video screens; but the other names became scrambled at once. There'd be time to unscramble them later, he knew.

Pomerantz went on, "That's the whole group. Six of us and Doc. And now you. Right out of high school, are you?"

"That's right."

"You'll be getting a crash course in xenobiology while you're here, which I suppose is all to the good. But mostly you'll be doing a lot of dumb odd jobs that the rest of us are too busy for. That's the penalty for low seniority here."

Bill grinned. "I don't mind. As long as I can be this close to the Old Martians—"

"It doesn't bother you at all to be errand boy for a bunch of kidnappers?" Pomerantz asked.

"Kidnappers? I don't follow. You mean, because you brought the Old Martians here from their native planet, and—"

"Skip it," said Pomerantz. "I used a foolish word."

"But—"

"*Skip it.*"

Bill decided not to push for an explanation. Pomerantz seemed ready enough to explode as it was. Bill knew in advance what the answer to his questions would be, too: "It's a long story." He meant to hear that story, sooner or later, since obviously something was troubling these people. Not now, though.

Pomerantz said, "Let's take a look at those dials. I want you to see what Sid Webster is doing, because you'll be doing it yourself before long. This is the reading for the temperature upstairs in the dwelling chamber. If it goes more than four degrees above or below freezing, a red light will flash, but we want to catch things before they get that bad. This meter shows atmospheric pressure—"

5

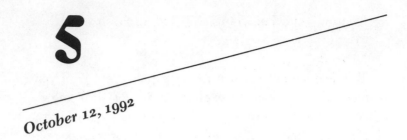

October 12, 1992

The seven scientists of the Mars Pavilion kept him too busy even to have time to think. In theory, employees of the Fair were supposed to work six hours a day, six days a week; but that theory didn't seem to go into operation until the Fair itself was open. Here in the final pre-opening days everyone was working double and triple time.

Bill was the only private in an army that otherwise consisted of six colonels and a general, and that was a headache. They all had work for him, work that had been accumulating during the weeks that the Mars Pavilion had been getting along without him. He found himself cleaning microscope slides for Dr. Chiang, nailing together a maze for the psychological experiments Dr. Sullivan and Nate Kuharich were doing, sorting computer printouts of Martian language samples for Dr. Milbank, listening to

Sid Webster recite what was supposed to be Martian poetry, slipping into the dwelling chamber to collect water pods for Lou Pomerantz, and proofreading the scientific reports that Dr. Martinson was writing. He also fought off reporters and other curious individuals trying to get an advance peek at the pavilion, supervised the workmen who were checking out the circuitry of the airlock doors, and spent three hours out of every twenty-four sitting in front of the environment monitors, making sure all was well upstairs. In his spare time he was allowed to explore the Fair Satellite—nearly all the pavilions were open to employees and journalists by now—but the trouble was that he never had much spare time. Work, meals, and sleep consumed about twenty-two hours out of every twenty-four, and he didn't have much energy left for sightseeing in the other two. When he was off duty he stumbled back to the dormitory, where, more often than not, Mel Salter and Nick Antonelli were pounding away on guitar and ocarina, so that even relaxation time was not very relaxing. Life became a blur of work, drab synthetic food, and patchy sleep.

But he was having the time of his life.

The Mars Pavilion was more than just a place of entertainment. It was a functioning xenobiological laboratory, the only one of its kind in the world. So far as the Fairgoing public was concerned, the important part of the pavilion was the glassed-in chamber in which the Old Martians could be viewed; but the real work was going on one level below. On Mars, conditions made proper observation of the Old Martians by scientists a difficult proposition, since research facilities on the red planet were primitive at best, and the xenobiologists had the further complication of being forced to conduct their work in a grim, inhospitable desert, carrying with them their own supplies of air and water.

Here, though, a small chunk of Mars had been transported intact, Martians and all. The dwelling chamber was full of sensing devices which relayed unique and invaluable data to the scientists in the laboratory below. For the first time it was possible to carry on continuous observations of the life-processes, habits, metabolism, and language of the Old Martians. A torrent of information poured constantly down. In the few weeks since the Old Martians had been living on the Fair Satellite, more had been learned about them than in the previous two years since the discovery of their kind. It was going to take years to digest and analyze the newly obtained data. Meanwhile, the six xenobiologists—each a specialist in some aspect of Old Martian life—tried to make the greatest possible use of their splendid research opportunity, while Dr. Martinson coordinated the entire project.

Bill did not get to know all seven of them equally well. Dr. Martinson, who had been so hostile at first and then so friendly, now became merely aloof; it was quite plain that he was too busy to give much time to Bill, and the only time Bill saw him was when some task had to be done. Bill likewise had little contact with Dr. Chiang, an older man preoccupied with his research into the cell structure of the Martian plants, or with Nate Kuharich, the shy, awkward assistant psychologist. But he found Lou Pomerantz interesting and appealing despite his explosive impatience, for Pomerantz had many of his own curiosities and attitudes, and in some ways seemed like an older version of himself, a vision of what he might become in another dozen years; he got along well with Dr. Milbank, the stoop-shouldered, nearsighted expert on the Martian language, who tried to teach him how to pronounce the harsh, whispery sounds of it; and he quickly became friendly with Sid Webster, the youngest of all the xenobiologists, only four years out of college himself and trying to wring from the Martians some scraps of their poetry and history.

All of them, though, allowed Bill to question them about their work, and answered as freely as time permitted. They appeared to regard him as the pavilion's mascot—earnest, friendly, eager to learn—and, though he sensed occasionally that they were making fun of him in a lighthearted way, he didn't mind at all. This was what he wanted most: to be close to some genuine xenobiologists, to watch them at work, above all to have first-hand experience with the Old Martians. Even before he entered college, he would have a closer acquaintance with the challenges of xenobiology than most graduate students had. Winning this contest entitled him to more than simply a year at the World's Fair; it gave him a running head start on his future.

Now and again he picked up clues that all was not exactly as it should be among the staff of the Mars Pavilion. That twice-repeated line about "a long story" was one such tip; Lou Pomerantz' careless and quickly retracted reference to the scientists as "a bunch of kidnappers" was another. Bill could detect hidden tensions, muffled conflicts in the pavilion. All seven of the xenobiologists appeared to be under a strain unrelated to the fatigue of their daily work. Something was bothering them. Bill thought he had a good idea what it was.

Some of them, at least, had guilty consciences over

bringing the Old Martians to the World's Fair.

The "kidnappers" remark would fit in there. So would the exaggerated precautions taken to make sure that the Old Martian's environment never varied from the right levels. And other small hints told Bill how worried the xenobiologists must be over the possibility that something might happen to the alien beings. But he asked no questions. He was too new here, and the subject was too sensitive. As a very junior member of the pavilion staff, he didn't think it was his place to probe such delicate matters.

Opening day was drawing near, now. The pace was frantic for nearly everyone on the Fair Satellite. It wasn't as bad at the Mars Pavilion as at some; the Mars Pavilion had been finished early, except for a few of the posters and exhibits, and the work there amounted to not much more than an exhausting series of final checkouts. At other pavilions, though, crews were toiling overtime and over-overtime to make up for earlier delays, confusions, and mistakes. Shuttle ships arrived every few minutes from Earth, bearing new exhibits and supplies. The whole Nigerian Pavilion had to be repainted at the end of September because a visiting Nigerian official disliked the color scheme; it reminded him, he said, of the colors of his country's flag before the last revolution. The electrical system of the Hall of the Worlds went out of commission during a special showing for a delegation of United Nations people, and had to be given a total going-over. A young computer technician accidentally cancelled the program for the film display in the German Federal Union Pavilion, and two experts had to be rocketed up from Earth on a day's notice to reprogram everything. And so it went—a desperate, frenzied race against time. Everyone on the

Fair Satellite was developing a look of glazed-eyed exhaustion as the 12th of October approached.

The place was filling up, too. Every day brought a new load of staff people: the ushers, guides, and other minor aides. Bill's third bunkmate arrived as scheduled on the first of October; he was part of the television relay crew that would be sending scenes from the Fair back to Earth. Bill almost never saw him, because his schedule had him sleeping when Bill was working, and vice versa. Not that anyone slept a great deal after October 1.

The ushering staff for the Mars Pavilion also started to show up in the first few days of October. There were eight ushers in all, four boys, four girls. The ushers, like their counterparts all over the Fair, were high school or college students whose families had enough pull to get them their jobs; they had no particular scientific reason for working for this pavilion. Bill, who was considered part of the research staff of the pavilion, no longer felt like the absolute bottom man of the outfit. Even though most of the ushers were older than he was, they respected him for his status as a "downstairs man," one who worked in the lab. It was not, after all, much of an achievement to stand around in a World's Fair uniform and shovel attendees from one room to the next, which was about all the ushers would be doing.

The entire group of ushers was on hand by October 4. The next day, the Mars Pavilion was finally opened to the press and to the rest of the Fair's personnel. Bill had never understood why the virtually completed pavilion had been closed all this time. One possibility was that the research staff just didn't want to be bothered by having outsiders in the pavilion; keeping the place shut gave them a month or two to work in privacy. But even that couldn't explain the top-security measures imposed on the pavilion. Surely it should have been possible to conduct important journalists like Roger Fancourt through the pavilion, or some of the diplomatic bigwigs who had been touring the Fair Satellite during the final weeks of construction. Yet nobody —no matter how well known or influential—had penetrated the barricades since the day the Old Martians had been installed in their dwelling chamber.

Bill got the answer, at last, only an hour before the first press showing. Lou Pomerantz solved the mystery for him.

"We kept the pavilion shut out of sheer cowardice," he said.

"I don't follow."

"We weren't sure whether the Old Martians would survive being transplanted here. It was a colossal gamble. If some of them died, we'd never hear the end of it. So we saw to it that no outsiders knew exactly how many Martians we had in here, or had a chance to learn to recognize particular ones. That gave us from August to early October to see if they'd live. If any of them died, the plan was to sneak others in from Mars as replacements."

"Without saying anything?"

"Without a word," Pomerantz admitted. "All done by sleight of hand—carry the dead Martians away, slip substitutes into the pavilion, and nobody the wiser."

"But that was—" Bill hesitated. "Not quite proper," he finished lamely.

"Dishonest is the word I think you were groping for."

Bill looked away uneasily. "I suppose, yes. Dishonest."

"It wasn't my idea," Pomerantz said heavily. "I had

nothing to do with it. There are times I wish I had nothing to do with any of this. But I guess it doesn't matter now. We made it through the trial period, and every Martian's in good health, so—"

"What if one of them dies now?" Bill asked. "There'll be no way of concealing it after the Fair's open."

"If it happens, it happens," Pomerantz said. "And we'll get blasted from one end of the scientific world to the other. As if we haven't been already. But it won't be my fault. I'll wash my hands of the whole mess. I—" He paused, as though realizing he had said much too much. "Listen, why do you worry so much, Hastings? The Old Martians aren't going to die on us. Suppose you go upstairs and see if the ushers need some help, or something."

The ushers had everything under control. It was just as well, because at the moment Bill had no help to offer them; he was too troubled by what Lou Pomerantz had said. It was no secret to him that there was plenty of cynicism and shadiness in the world, but he hadn't expected to find it among people like this. He had thought someone like Dr. Martinson would be above such a maneuver. Would it really be so damaging to his scientific reputation if some of the Old Martians died while on exhibit at the Fair? Yes, Bill decided, it probably would be. Even so, it didn't seem right for him to keep outsiders from seeing the pavilion while he tested the sturdiness of the little creatures.

The scanner screens showed a vast line forming in front of the pavilion. The master computer had decided on the order in which the press people would be let in; by the end of the day every journalist then at the Fair would have viewed the pavilion, and beginning the next day the Fair personnel would have their chance, so that everyone could see the Old Martians before the general public started to arrive. Since this was the first test of the viewing procedure, the whole staff was a little on edge. They had rehearsed everything for days, now, using the off-duty ushers and some of the xenobiologists as the "crowd," but the real pattern would not become clear until heavy traffic began. The flow charts were computer-designed to feed people through the series of air-tight chambers in such a way that most of the locks remained sealed at any one time. Each group that reached the innermost chamber would be given ten minutes to watch the Old Martians, and then would be hustled toward the exit.

The problem that worried all the pavilion people was what would happen if the onlookers refused to leave when their ten minutes were up. Dr. Martinson hoped that the natural tendency of people in a crowd to do as they were told would keep everything moving smoothly—but some of the others, especially Dr. Milbank, had their doubts. The public's fascination with the Old Martians was so great, Milbank argued, that it was going to be necessary to post guards to force the crowds out.

The ushers took their positions, one in each of the four outer chambers. Bill stationed himself in the outermost chamber to follow the developments. The main door opened; people came bubbling in until the computer, measuring the audience in terms of volume, decided that the room was full. A red light flashed over the door, alerting the usher, who politely but forcefully cut off the inflow and allowed the door to close.

Now the narration tape began to play. "Welcome to the Mars Pavilion," a resonant voice declared. "You are about to witness the most remarkable exhibit ever shown to twentieth-century man: the living inhabitants of another planet, housed in their own natural environment, functioning as they do on their native world. First, though, some words about the planet of Mars—"

All this was strictly a stalling maneuver. Nobody who came here really wanted to hear a lecture about Mars; but something had to be done to amuse those on line while the lucky ones ahead were watching the Old Martians. So each of the four airlock chambers gave its captive audience five minutes of information: a general introduction to Mars, then an account of the climate and physical appearance of the planet, a discussion of Martian archaeology, and an account of the discovery of the Old Martians themselves. Finally, the last door opened, yielding a ten-minute view of the dwelling chamber to complete the half-hour visit to the pavilion.

Bill stayed with the initial group as it progressed inward. Bill, who had heard the background lectures a hundred times apiece during the checkouts of the last few weeks, began silently to recite the texts from memory, a sentence ahead of the narrator, to fight off the boredom. But at last the door to the dwelling chamber swung open.

Instead of looking at the Old Martians, Bill watched the audience. The expressions of awe, wonder, astonishment, delight, and excitement were fascinating to behold. Some of the women looked frightened, though, as if they were realizing for the first time that the universe held complicated forms of life that had no connection whatever with Earth. Some of the newsmen looked bothered by the strangeness or the smallness or the fragility of the Old Martians. Some seemed disappointed, though Bill could not imagine why. And some—there always had to be a few of that sort, he thought—merely looked bored. The range of reactions was instructive, following as it did a mathematically perfect curve from the yawning minority at one end to the totally awe-smitten at the other.

One hurdle proved not to be so difficult to leap after all. At the end of ten minutes the exit door opened and the narrator boomed, "We hope that you have enjoyed your visit to the caves of Mars, and that as you leave you will reflect on the miracle of life in the universe, the possibility that other worlds yet unvisited by man may yield even greater surprises than—"

And the audience began obediently to shuffle out.

Bill remained behind. He watched the exit door close again, and the door at the other side of the chamber open, admitting the second group to the viewing area. During the next minute doors would be sliding back and forth all through the pavilion as each group was moved one stage closer to the Old Martians. So far, so good, he thought. The show was going to work out.

Over the next few days, thousands of eager visitors passed through the Mars Pavilion. Just about everyone who worked at the Fair managed to find half an hour off to see it, and there was never any time when less than a thousand people were lined up outside. Some of the pressure was off, now, and Bill had a chance to tour the rest of the Fair. He wandered everywhere—to the Hall of the Worlds, finally in good working order; to the amusement midway, with its concessions, its sideshows, its robot barkers; to the tridim sensie shows, sponsored by the Hollywood studios, where you not only saw the action, you smelled and felt and tasted it too; to the pavilions of the great corporations and the important nations; to the fountain and the reflecting pool; to the windows onto the universe.

The pavilion restaurants were in operation, and he treated himself to a couple of fancy meals as a contrast to the dreary fare he had been getting in the staff cafeteria. They were the most expensive dinners he had ever had in his life, but they were worth it. One night he dined at the French pavilion with Mel Salter and Nick Antonelli, and at Mel's prodding allowed himself to order snails for his appetizer. When the snails came, he stared at the little metal tray for a long while before he could bring himself to start eating. Mel and Nick watched him, looking amused and snide and superior, and in the end he grasped one shell with the little clamp, fished out the snail, and ate it without looking at it.

"Hey, it's *good!*" he said a moment later, amazed.

The next night he ate at the Nigerian Pavilion, where he parted with close to a week's pay for an African feast lasting two hours. This time his companions were Lou Pomerantz and Sid Webster, and Bill said very little, listening to their talk of projects still to be carried out. Just as the main course reached the table, Pomerantz abruptly stiffened, his face darkening with anger. Bill noticed that people were turning their heads all over the glittering dining room.

"There he is," Pomerantz muttered. "Claude Regan himself!"

Through the room ran the same hushed words: Regan, Regan, Regan! Bill looked around and saw that a group of imposingly dressed and obviously very important people had entered the dining room. There were three Africans in flowing, colorful tribal robes, and a couple of distinguished-looking men in business suits who might have been bankers or congressmen, and some extraordinarily glamorous women wearing the new sprayon fashions; and there was Claude Regan. The president of Global Factors was the least impressive person in the group, at first glance: small, compact, lean, with a thick mop of red hair and blue, almost faded-looking eyes. He looked no more than thirty years old, and he seemed overshadowed by those around him. But a second glance left no doubt about who the central figure of the party really was. Regan had an inner radiance, a glow of self-confidence and strength, a look of power and authority that belied his small size and ordinary-looking features. This was *his* show, *his* satellite, *his* planet in the sky, and no one could doubt that for an instant. Here he was, the night before the official opening, looking upon his works and finding them good.

The dining room relaxed as the Regan party was shown to its table. Only Lou Pomerantz remained tense, glowering across the room at Regan in unmistakable fury.

"Something wrong, Lou?" Bill asked.

"I hope he chokes on his soup!"

Sid Webster said in tones of warning, "Cut it out, Lou. People can hear you."

"So what? I said, I hope he chokes on his soup. If ever there was a man who deserved—"

"Stop it," Webster said. "Don't make a scene or they'll throw us out, Lou!"

Bill was baffled. He knew that there were people who disliked Claude Regan because he was ambitious, because he was ruthless, because he was so powerful, or simply because he was worth a billion dollars at the age of 35. But Bill couldn't understand the intense, deeply personal sort of hatred that Lou Pomerantz was showing. Claude Regan had always seemed too remote from ordinary people to hate; it was like trying to hate the Moon. Besides, creating a World's Fair of this sort was a mighty accomplishment, and without Claude Regan's drive, energy, and imagination they would all be somewhere else this evening.

"That's exactly it," Pomerantz said a few minutes later, when Bill pressed him for an explanation. "Without Regan we'd all be somewhere else tonight. You'd be on Earth, and Sid and I would probably be doing research on Mars, and our six Old Martians would be on Mars too—where they belong."

"You sound as though you hold it against him personally that the Old Martians are here," Bill said.

"I do! I do! That's the whole thing! Don't you see, Bill this is all one of Regan's filthy schemes? This exploitation of science, this perversion of science? He—"

"Lou, *please* keep your voice down," Sid Webster begged. "You're talking loud enough for Regan to hear you all the way across the room."

"So what? Let him fire me, if he likes. Listen, Bill, maybe you aren't aware of it, but as of the first day of 1992 this fair was about to fold up. Billions of dollars had been spent, and the advance sale was next to nothing. People weren't booking reservations. Regan took a poll and found out that half the population was afraid to get into a spaceship and go anywhere, and the other half didn't think the Fair Satellite itself was going to be a safe place to be. And the third half didn't want to spend the money. A trip to the Fair might cost a thousand bucks, figuring all the costs, and—"

"There can't be any third half," Bill said.

Pomerantz ignored him. "It looked like the Fair would go bankrupt. The exhibitors and concessionaires mostly have contracts calling for rent reductions if advance ticket sales fall below a certain point. Not only would the Fair's profit be cut to nothing, but it wouldn't even be able to pay interest on its own bonds. And there are billions of dollars of bonds. The Regan staff discussed the situation and decided that the Fair had to come up with some extra-special attraction, something that people couldn't possibly get to see at an amusement park on Earth, something that would pull people to the Fair like a magnet. There was only one possible answer."

"The Martians," Bill said.

"The Martians. Exactly. He appropriated fifty million bucks to duplicate the environment of a Martian cave up here, and went to Mars personally to collect his exhibit. Old bring'em-back-alive Regan. I'll bet you thought the Old Martians were protected by United Nations law, or something like that."

"Well, yes."

"They aren't. The U.N. is still debating it, but as of now anybody who feels like it can go up there and do what he wants with them. Shoot them and mount their heads on a trophy wall. Or catch them as zoo specimens, the way Regan did." Pomerantz glared coldly across the room. "I'll tell you how he did it, too. First he went before the Mars-port Legislature and let it be known that Global Factors was willing to pick up the cost for some new atmosphere-generating equipment for the colony. Say, twenty million bucks' worth. Then he added that he'd like to borrow half a dozen Old Martians for a little while, as World's Fair exhibits, and of course they'd be treated well and kept under scientific supervision and returned in good health when the Fair closed. The Marsport Legislature passed a special law okaying it. Why not? He was offering to rent the Old Martians for twenty million—and they knew they couldn't really stop him from just taking them, anyway. Next he went shopping for his Martians. He toured some caves, picked out a family group, two adults and one child of each sex, and explained that he'd like them to live at the World's Fair for a while. You can imagine how much of that they understood. Finally the Martians got the idea that he meant to take them away somewhere, and told him they didn't want to go. But he was insistent. These Martians, as you've seen, are a passive people. They aren't fighters. They meet every crisis with a shrug. So they shrugged, and Regan took them. Meanwhile he had an engineering crew in here, setting up an exact duplicate of the Martian environment. It was ready by late June. On July 1 he announced that there were going to be live Old Martians at the Fair. By the end of July, the first three months of the Fair were completely sold out. There wasn't a seat to be had on any flights to the Fair, and no accommodations on the Fair Satellite at all. Regan's gamble had paid off. Everybody wants to see Martians, but hardly anyone can afford to go to Mars to see them. Thanks to Claude Regan, they would be only 50,000 miles from Earth, instead of 50,000,000. And no one was unhappy about it except a few crackpot scientists. And the Old Martians themselves, I guess, but who pays any attention to them?"

Bill said, "Mind a personal question, Lou?"

"Go ahead."

"If you're so angry about Claude Regan's having brought the Old Martians here, what are you doing here yourself? Aren't you giving a kind of approval to the whole thing by taking part in it?"

Pomerantz smiled sourly. "Now we come to the heart of things. It's a long—"

"I know," Bill said. "It's a long story. I want to hear it."

"It isn't really that long. You probably weren't aware of it, Bill, but a committee of leading xenobiologists spent most of last summer fighting Regan's maneuver. There were petitions, advertisements in scientific periodicals, letter-writing campaigns, the works. Doc Martinson was the head of the committee, and—"

"Doc Martinson? But here he is working for Regan's Fair!"

"Exactly," Pomerantz said. "I was active on the committee, and so was Sid here, and everybody else on the pavilion research staff except Chiang and Milbank. We fought Regan with everything we had. Unfortunately, we didn't have very much. We couldn't even afford a video commercial to reach the general public. So we lost."

"And then you joined the enemy," Bill said.

Pomerantz nodded. "We joined the enemy, precisely."

"But why? By being here, you lend respectability to what Regan did, and—"

"We came here," Pomerantz said, "either out of idealism or selfishness, I'm not sure which. We told ourselves that since there was no way to prevent Regan from kidnapping the Martians and bringing them to the Fair, it was our moral responsibility as scientists to see to it that a top crew of xenobiologists was here to take care of these precious and irreplaceable alien beings. Right? Also it happened to be an unparalleled scientific opportunity for us. We could get closer to the Martians, study them with more continuity, than we possibly could on Mars. Regan was offering us a fully equipped laboratory, all expenses paid, and a group of Martians under ideal observing conditions. At first none of us would touch the deal. Then Doc Martinson announced that he felt obliged, as a ranking man in his field, to make sure the Old Martians received proper treatment here. Once he joined Regan the rest of us followed along. In the end there were more than fifty applicants for the six research posts at the Fair."

"Wait a minute," Bill said. "Which counted more: your desire to protect the six Old Martians, or your eagerness to get a shot at the research opportunities here?"

"We don't know," Pomerantz said moodily. "We don't know. That's the agony. Did we sell out to Regan, or were our motives decent? Were we tempted by the research opportunities into betraying our own ideals? Should we have gone on denouncing Regan, even it it meant letting the six Martians get inferior care and die? Bill, there's more to this science business than microscopes and computers, believe me. There's a moral thing, all the time. We're sick over it, all seven of us. Can't you see it in our faces?"

"Of course I can. The strain, the tension—but I didn't understand why."

"Now you know," Pomerantz said. "And now eat your food before it gets any colder. None of this is really your worry. I just wanted you to see why I got worked up when Claude Regan walked in."

Bill ate without paying much attention to his food. Yes, he saw. He saw more than he had ever suspected, and wondered if he could really understand the dilemma of scientists who had let themselves become part of a project they despised. Did Lou Pomerantz really hate Claude Regan so much—or was his real hatred directed against himself? Regan was just an operator, a wheeler-dealer, a businessman trying to put on a profitable show; probably in his own mind Regan saw nothing wrong with having brought the Old Martians to the Fair. But Pomerantz and the other scientists were in a far more complex position, unable to decide whether it was concern for the Martians or just plain opportunism that had caused them to take part.

Pomerantz' long outburst cast a pall over the rest of the meal. None of them said much, except when the staggeringly huge check arrived. As they went out, Bill stared closely at Claude Regan, fixing in his mind the image of the man about whom such controversies swirled. Regan looked up. His eyes met Bill's and locked on them for a long, uncomfortable moment. Then he smiled, a smile of such dazzling charm that Bill was thrown into confusion, and rushed forward to catch up with Pomerantz and Sid Webster.

The Fair Satellite was an edgy, uneasy place that night. The last-minute work was finished; the celebrities were beginning to arrive for the Opening Day ceremonies; in a few more hours the 1992 Columbian Exposition would be thrown open to the world. After Bill left the two xenobiologists he walked from level to level, roaming the Fair for hours, moving at random along the ramps and corridors. Thousands of others were doing the same thing. None of the pavilions was open, now, although lights were on in many as the exhibitors ran through every detail one last time. But no one could relax, no one could go to sleep; everyone was out in the same sort of restless prowl.

Bill caught sight of Nick Antonelli towering above the crowd outside the Brazilian Pavilion, and waved to him; when he drew closer, he was a little surprised to see his bunkmate arm-in-arm with Emily Blackman. They smiled at each other—the quick, empty smile of nervousness— and then Nick and Emily were swept on in the throng. Much later in the night Bill came to the Mars Pavilion; it was shut tight, of course, and he could not get in without two other members of the staff to press their fingers to the scanner plate. He stood in front of it for a while, thinking of the small, strange creatures in their glass-walled chamber at the heart of the building.

The chime of midnight sounded through the Fair Satellite.

It was now October 12, 1992.

Five hundred years before, at two hours past midnight, a cannon had boomed out across the quiet Caribbean, and a five-week journey across the uncharted Atlantic came to its end. A sailor cried out, *"Tierra! Tierra!"* as he sighted land. A Genoese sea-captain named Cristoforo Colombo thereby attained a permanent place in the history of exploration.

Now, far from Earth, across a very different kind of sea, the discovery of that New World was about to be commemorated on an even newer world. Bill Hastings walked slowly back to his dormitory to catch a few hours of sleep, if he could. Tomorrow would be a big day. The 1992 World's Fair was at last beginning.

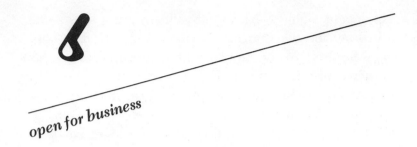

Shortly after dawn, Eastern Standard Time, three small spaceships soared skyward from spaceports on Earth. The World's Fair publicity office had named them the *Niña*, the *Pinta*, and the *Santa Maria*, which Bill thought was a little on the heavy-handed side. They bore the dignitaries who were to make the first day of the Fair such a glittering event.

The *Santa Maria*, as the flagship, carried the most resplendent cargo of all: the Secretary-General of the United Nations, the President of the United States of America, the Premier of the United States of Europe, and the heads of such powerful nations as the Soviet Union, the People's Republic of China, Brazil, the West African Federation, Argentina, the Congo. Kings and prime ministers, actors and musicians, athletes and financiers—all had come to to see the official opening of the 1992 Columbian Exposition. Attendance on the first day was by invitation only, and the guest-list was spectacular.

Bill was not the only one who asked himself whether some equally spectacular disaster might be in the making. Never before in the world's history had so many important people been gathered in one place that was so vulnerable. Was there ever a better setting for an assassination conspiracy? If some madmen got hold of a nuclear-tipped warhead and sent it streaking toward the Fair Satellite, virtually the entire leadership of the world would be removed in a single stroke.

There were plenty of rumors of just such a thing, Bill knew. Of course, the predictions of disaster were probably so much jetblast and nothing more. Claude Regan had a multitude of enemies—most of them jealous business rivals —who would be delighted to see Regan, Global Factors, and the World's Fair all fall on their faces. Deliberate stories of impending catastrophe had been circulating ever since the Fair was announced, in the hope of keeping attendance low and forcing Regan's gaudy project into bankruptcy. For a while those frightening tales had achieved their purpose; only the coup of bringing the Old Martians to the Fair had created a demand for tickets. Even now the whispers of doom could occasionally be heard, and it was hard not to take them seriously at least some of the time. There were enough cranks in the world to make even the wildest threat something to fear.

But thoughts of disaster faded as the Opening Day ceremonies began. Loudspeakers in every pavilion carried the speeches that the honored guests were delivering.

". . . a symbol of the dynamic energy, hard work, and far-sighted vision that is so uniquely American. . . ."

That was Secretary-General Hannikainen, praising the planners of the Fair.

". . . five centuries of adventure culminate here today, in this spectacular recapitulation of the American dream. . . ."

President Hammond, longwinded as usual.

". . . a stunning scientific achievement, an historic high-water mark in man's conquest of his environment. . . ."

Premier Falaise of Europe, sounding terribly bored.

The speeches went on and on. Bill fidgeted and twitched. He was sitting in the laboratory under the Mars Pavilion, watching the monitor dials. The screen showed him the Old Martians just above, entirely unaware of the festivities taking place all about them.

Each of the world leaders had been given five minutes to speak, but naturally some of them went over their quota, and there was no way of shutting them up. The religious invocations had taken a long time too. The Pope had decided at the last minute not to come, but he had sent an Apostolic Delegate; blessings also were delivered by a rabbi, a Presbyterian minister chosen by lot to represent all the non-Catholic Christian denominations, and an assortment of Hindu, Moslem, and Buddhist leaders. By the time they were through it was impossible to doubt that the good will of Heaven would shine upon the Fair.

And then, just when it seemed the ceremonies would never end, Claude Regan rose to speak. He said quietly, "There's not much I care to add after what's already been said. I simply want to extend to the whole universe, on behalf of the Americas, my invitation to come and help us celebrate our five-hundredth birthday. That's all. I now officially declare the 1992 Columbian Exposition to be open."

There was applause. Regan snipped the silk ribbon. The celebrities thronged forward.

The ceremony had been held outside the Hall of the Worlds, not far from the Mars Pavilion and the pavilion of Global Factors. A special showing at the Mars Pavilion had been arranged for the very highest level of dignitaries. The whole scientific staff of the pavilion was going to be on hand at the dwelling chamber—all except Nate Kuharich. Someone had to watch the monitor dials downstairs, and Nate had volunteered, probably because his overwhelming shyness left him with little desire to face the global potentates.

Dr. Martinson led the way upstairs.

The series of lectures in the outer chambers was skipped. The celebrities would be admitted as rapidly as the sequence of opening and closing airlocks would permit. So in a short time the final door opened, and Bill saw a dozen of the world's most familiar faces just beyond it. The great ones entered the chamber and scrambled like schoolboys for good positions at the viewing window, while poker-faced security guards quietly arranged themselves along the chamber's walls.

"Remarkable," the Secretary-General observed.

"Incredible," declared the President of the United States.

"Such wonderful little gnomes!" commented Chancellor Schmidt of the German Federal Union.

Dr. Martinson had prepared a little speech of welcome and explanation; but he was no more than sixty seconds into it when it became apparent to everyone that the dignitaries were paying no attention. They were staring at the Old Martians as though the alien beings were a family of unusually lively chimpanzees; and they were totally absorbed by the scene beyond the glass. The Soviet Premier was making funny faces in clumsy imitation of the features of the Martians. The President of Brazil was rapping on the glass, trying to get one of the young Martians to turn around. The wife of President Hammond of the United States was making gurgling and cooing sounds. Dr. Martinson wisely decided to abridge his speech; Bill, who had been through twenty rehearsals of it, was startled when the scientist abruptly leaped from his fifth paragraph to his next-to-last one, skipping a great deal that should have come in between. Meanwhile the world's leaders went right on trying to make the Old Martians notice them, as if Dr. Martinson hadn't told them that the glass gave one-way vision. It was quite a spectacle, Bill thought. He wondered what the Old Martians would make of it all if they really could see through the glass. Would they be able to tell that these were the mightiest men in the world? Would it matter to them at all if they knew?

Suddenly Bill became aware of the small, lean figure of Claude Regan practically at his elbow. Regan said, "I've seen you before, haven't I?"

Bill was too astounded to do anything more intelligent than open his mouth and gape.

"I remember," Regan went on smoothly. "At the Nigerian restaurant last night. You were staring at me as if I came from Mars."

"Well—I—uh—I mean—"

"Don't apologize. Everyone stares at me. I'm used to

it. You're on the research staff here, are you?"

"Yes, sir."

"What's your specialty?"

"None, exactly," Bill blurted. "That is—well, I'm not really a scientist. I'm just out of high school, in fact."

"Oh?"

"It was the essay contest, sir. You know, Life on Other Worlds. I was—well, that is—the winner."

"The essay contest," Regan said in a dreamy way. His eyes closed for a moment, and it seemed to Bill that wheels were clicking behind Regan's forehead as though in some vast computer. "Hastings," Regan said after a pause. "Hastings. John Hastings? No, William. For William the Conqueror, I suppose. A very fine essay, too, William. You really do think we'll discover living beings on Pluto, eh?"

Bill was so amazed that Regan knew of him, knew his name, had read his essay, that once again he could find no words. He wanted desperately to say something profound, learned, witty, and memorable, but all he could do was knot his hands together miserably behind his back and grin a foolish, sickly grin.

Regan seemed accustomed to having people go mute on him. In an easy and charming way he picked up the conversation just as though Bill had replied, and said, "I'm sure Pluto has all sorts of surprises for us. If I have anything to say about it, we'll be exploring it sooner than most people expect. And perhaps you'll be going along, William." He winked. "Keep up the good work."

And, favoring Bill with one last glittering smile, he turned away and slid gracefully into the conversation between Secretary-General Hannikainen and Chairman Ch'ien of China.

The high officials left the Mars Pavilion a few minutes later. Now the more ordinary celebrities were being admitted. Bill activated the staff exit panel in the wall and slipped out, even though some of the most famous sensie stars and rocket-polo heroes were coming in. He didn't feel like facing any more of the famous just now.

The one-sided conversation with Claude Regan had left him shaky with excitement. A Pluto expedition? Really? And was Regan serious about letting him take part?

Of course not, Bill decided. It was just some of the well-known Regan charm at work. The man was a manipulator of people; it was his business to know which buttons to push to make a person fall in line. With such skills he had made himself one of the wealthiest and most powerful men on Earth. With just that sort of razzle-dazzle, no doubt, he had persuaded the Marsport legislators to let him walk off with half a dozen Old Martians. Yes, Mr. Regan. Of course, Mr. Regan. Take all the Martians you need, Mr. Regan. Would you like one of our moons, too? Anything you want, Mr. Regan.

It was hard to resist a man like that.

Bill had completely overlooked, while talking to him, that this was the terrible villain Lou Pomerantz had glared at so murderously last night. This was the kidnapper of defenseless Martians, the vanquisher of outraged scientists, the unscrupulous and ruthless operator who would seize anything in the universe that would help his World's Fair show a profit. Bill understood now how Regan had been able to get the petition-signing, protest-letter-writing xenobiologists to join his side. Money alone hadn't done it. But by taking the trouble to learn a man's name and something about him, to approach him on a personal level and hit him hard with the news that Claude Regan cared about him, Regan could win anyone over. Lou Pomerantz, Bill noticed, had pulled away into a shadowy corner of the room when Regan came in, as if he was afraid of having the Regan treatment worked on *him*.

One by one, the pavilion staff came downstairs to the lab level. Everyone looked vastly relieved. The worst was over; the celebrities were gone; now they could get back to their research.

For Bill it meant the start of something like a regular routine. No longer did he have to put in hours of overtime everyday. He still would spend nine or ten hours a day at the pavilion, though. The trouble was only eight staffers, Bill included, were qualified to watch the monitor dials, and so he had to continue to take his three-hour stints there, while trying to do his other work at a different time. It wasn't so bad, though. While in front of the dials he could still talk to the others in the lab and follow what they were doing. Monitoring became a chore only when he drew one of the late-night shifts, as happened two or three times a week. Usually one or two of the other scientists were in the lab with him, but the dawn shift tended to be a dreary battle against slumber.

There were other little inconveniences, too, having to do with the intricate locking system of the pavilion. Pomerantz, Kuharich, and Webster all needed a triple fingerprint combination to get in; and when only two of the three were available at some odd hour, they usually hunted for Bill, rather than for one of the senior scientists. He grew accustomed to having Pomerantz and Webster or Webster and Kuharich or Kuharich and Pomerantz show up apologetically at his dorm room to awaken him. Sometimes a senior staffer, Dr. Milbank or Dr. Chiang, who needed only one other fingerprint pattern on the scanner plate to get in, would come to fetch him for the same favor. It made Bill feel conscious of sharing an important responsibility, but it was also a nuisance.

Nuisances like that could be tolerated. The important thing was that he was doing the work he had always dreamed of doing. Who needed sleep, anyway?

Each day he penetrated a little deeper into the mysteries of xenobiology. Each of the scientists at the pavilion seemed to want to convert him—some more obviously than the others—to his own special branch of the subject. Dr. Milbank, for example, went out of his way to persuade Bill to go in for xenolinguistics. "Until we can speak their language fluently," Millbank said, "we won't have any idea what Martian life is all about."

Bill wasn't entirely convinced of that. We know a whole lot about the biology of flatworms, he reflected, and we can't understand a word of what they say. But he kept such thoughts to himself, paid close attention to the instruction Dr. Milbank gave him, and discovered, to his pleasure and surprise, that he had something of a knack for Old Martian. He mastered the few phrases that were understood and spent some time listening to tapes of incomprehensible sentences, searching as Dr. Milbank did for patterns of sounds out of which some sense might be wrung. For a while Bill was tempted seriously to take up xenolinguistics as his eventual specialty, even though it really wasn't a biological science.

Then Lou Pomerantz took over, drawing Bill back into his usual field of interests by showing him the results of his research into the metabolism of the Old Martians. Pomerantz was trying to find out what kept the little creatures going—how they got nourishment from their plants, how rapidly they grew, how long they lived. He analyzed the chemical content of the water in the Martion water pods, measured the rate of their breathing and the pace of their blood circulation through remote telemetry, and carried on a dozen similar experiments. Like Dr. Milbank, Pomerantz was convinced that his particular work was the basis of all understanding of the Old Martians, and what the others were doing was mere trimming. "Here we have a chance to study a race that evolved under totally alien conditions," Pomerantz argued. "Evolution has designed these beings to respond to an environment remote from anything we know. If we can learn exactly how those alien bodies of theirs work, it'll not only be scientifically valuable in itself, but it'll help us gain a deeper knowledge of how evolution has functioned on Earth as well. For the first time we'll have some points of comparison with an outside system." Bill found himself agreeing completely. What could be more valuable than knowing how life sustained itself on so inhospitable a world as Mars?

Pomerantz was hampered by the general unwillingness of the Old Martians to let themselves be examined closely by Earthmen. He did as much as he could with the long-range sensor devices planted all over the dwelling chamber, but it would have been simpler for him to go to work on the Martians with thermometers, electrocardiographs, respiration analyzers, and other body-contact instruments. He was hoping that Milbank's linguistic research would progress to the point where it would be possible to explain the purpose of the metabolic experiments to the Martians and win their cooperation, but he had little faith that that would happen soon.

The work of Dr. Chiang dovetailed neatly with that of Pomerantz. Chiang, too, was studying Martian metabolism, although from a different angle. He was concentrating on the puzzle of the Martian plants, seeking to know how they manufactured the oxygen and food that kept the Old Martians alive. He was a silent, self-contained man, who appeared to regard conversation as a major effort; but yet he took the trouble several times to show Bill interesting aspects of the cellular structure of the plants. Chiang did not quite say it in so many words, but the implication was there: my work is significant and will reveal a great deal, in time.

Dr. Sullivan and Nate Kuharich, who were working together on an analysis of Martian psychology, were firmly convinced that theirs was the key specialty. Dr. Sullivan, a forceful and aggressive woman in her early forties, was most direct about it. "We've got the solution to every problem in psychology in that room upstairs. At last we can define a human being, because the Martians give us a yardstick to measure ourselves by. They're intelligent, civilized, have a spoken language, a cultural tradition—and they're wholly alien. By studying their reactions to situations, we can begin to understand what our reactions mean."

It was the same argument Lou Pomerantz had used: know thyself better by knowing strangers. Comprehend human patterns—of psychology, of metabolism, of anything—more clearly by analyzing alien patterns. He wasn't sure you needed Martians for such research, though;

dolphins ought to be just as revealing. But he couldn't deny Dr. Sullivan's other point, that here was a chance to get in on the start of an absolutely new science, xenopsychology. Bill didn't doubt that the Old Martians were going to be subjected to batteries of psychological tests to the end of their days; but he didn't think it was really the field for him.

Sid Webster made only a token attempt to win him as a disciple. His specialty was a different branch of xenolinguistics; where Dr. Milbank was trying to determine the meaning of individual Martian words and perhaps the structure of Martian grammar, Sid was several steps beyond that, attempting to assemble bits of Martian literature. Since so little of the Martian language was understood, he worked mostly with the English-speaking Martians in the dwelling chamber, patiently winning their friendship and hoping to wangle from them some details of their culture. He had actually persuaded one of the Martians to recite a long epic poem that supposedly dealt with the vanished days of Martian greatness, millions of years ago, before the retreat to the caves. Unfortunately, the Martian refused to translate the poem, and Dr. Milbank and Sid together were able to understand less than a dozen words out of many thousands. Still, the work was down on tape, and perhaps someday it could be decoded. Bill wondered if the whole thing might be a collection of nonsense syllables—a Martian version of a practical joke—but he avoided suggesting any such thing to Sid Webster, who took his work very seriously.

The scientist who had the greatest difficulty getting anything accomplished was Dr. Martinson, the top man. He was attempting to study the physical anatomy of the

Old Martians, to discover the mysteries that lay beneath their coarse gray skins. He had begun his work with the skeletons of long-dead Martians found years ago by archaeologists; but learning something about the internal organs of living Martians was proving a major challenge. Not only were the Martians reluctant to let him examine them, but they wholly refused to permit him to dissect their dead. It was a religious matter. On Mars, tradition called for the dead to be placed in a posture of sleep within a cave and left undisturbed, so that over the centuries the body would slowly decay and return to the environment. To mutilate a body in any way—as in an anatomical dissection—would be a desecration. To remove even a sliver of skin from a corpse, let alone the internal organs, was a serious offense against nature. Every molecule of the dead one's body must be permitted to decay naturally.

"Anatomists had an easier time of it in the Middle Ages," Dr. Martinson complained. "Dissecting corpses was forbidden then, too—but at least the Church allowed executed criminals to be cut up. The Martians don't have any criminals. And they wouldn't let me cut them up even if they did."

He compared himself to Andreas Vesalius, the great sixteenth-century anatomist, who had had to sneak into graveyards by night to get the cadavers he needed for his research. Working in cooperation with archaeologists on Mars, Dr. Martinson had obtained and dissected half a dozen corpses of Old Martians dead anywhere from one to eight hundred years. That gave him at least a rough working knowledge of Martian anatomy, since in the dry, almost airless, practically bacteria-free surroundings of an abandoned Martian cave it took thousands of years for advanced decay to set in. But it was hard on his conscience to skulk around stealing corpses that way, even though he doubted that any living Martians would ever discover the thefts; and he could learn more from one newly dead Martian than from a hundred ancient corpses. There seemed no way to get such a specimen without giving mortal offense; even so, Dr. Martinson had contrived to achieve remarkable knowledge of the structure of the Martian body.

The gentle, underplayed rivalry among the scientists for Bill's interest had its amusing aspects. It had benefits, too; for the researchers were no longer giving him humble cleanup jobs to do, but were taking him more closely into their work, involving him with their research itself. But it was also a trifle troublesome to be wooed this way; Dr. Sullivan was jealous of the time Bill spent with Dr. Milbank, Lou Pomerantz begrudged his activities with the psychology team, Dr. Milbank looked regretful when Bill excused himself to go to Dr. Chiang, and so on around the circle.

One night after leaving the Mars Pavilion he found himself discussing the situation with Emily Blackman. The Fair was in its fourth week, and business was booming; Bill had spent eleven hours in the Mars Pavilion that day, two of them assisting Pomerantz in programming the computer with metabolic analyses, and two of them reading Martian verbs—maybe adjectives—to Dr. Milbank. He felt frayed and numb from too much hard work. As he passed the Hall of the Worlds on his way to the down-ramp, Emily appeared and fell into step beside him. When she commented on his look of fatigue, he said, "I know.

They're running me ragged. Each one's trying to convert me to his own field, and I'm being given full exposure to the toughest problems of every xenobiological specialty. There are times I envy the ushers here. They don't have to think at all."

"You ought to be flattered," Emily said.

"Well, it is flattering, I guess. But exhausting, too. I have to give equal time to all of them, or they get jealous and pout."

"Why do you think they're so keen on impressing you?"

"To justify the importance of their own work, I suppose," Bill said. "Each one can't help but think that what he's doing is more valuable. But the only proof is in the way a newcomer like me responds."

"So they're really flattering themselves, and not you, when they go after you?"

"In a way, that's it," he agreed. "Winning my enthusiasm is a challenge to them. I don't really count as an individual—heck, I'm a kid right out of high school, so how can they care much about my alleged scientific abilities? They're just trying to test the attractiveness of their own specialties." He frowned. "You know, when I put it in those terms, I feel sort of deflated."

"You're the one who put it that way," Emily pointed out. "I didn't say a thing. Besides, maybe they really do want to recruit you for your own sake. That essay of yours is more highly regarded than you may realize. Why, just last week Claude Regan asked to have a thousand copies of it run off."

"What for?"

She shrugged. "How would I know? He called Mr. Palisander and said to dig the essay out and print it up.

98

So we did, and one of Regan's flunkeys went off with the whole stack. Maybe those scientists don't think you're just a high school kid."

Bill laughed. "As a matter of fact, I'm about to win the 1992 Nobel Prize. Right?"

"Who told you? It was supposed to be a secret!" she cried. She laughed too, and thrust her arm into his, and they went running past the Global Factors Pavilion to the downramp.

He was seeing much more of Emily these days than he had ever expected. True, she had appeared to show a good deal of interest in him during his first few days aboard the Fair Satellite. But in the frenzied final weeks before Opening Day he had had nothing more than occasional glimpses of her, and most of the times he had seen her she had been in the company of his towering bunkmate, Nick Antonelli. Now, suddenly, Emily seemed to be haunting him. Four times in a single week he caught sight of her coming out of the Hall of the Worlds just as he happened past. Each time she claimed to have been visiting her cousin Mel Salter there; but each time, also, she and Bill went strolling off together to tour the Fair for the next hour or so. She turned up in the cafeteria when he was there, too. Even though he took his meals at unpredictable hours, he met Emily there more often than not, as though she were keeping a scanner watch on him and making sure to be in the cafeteria when he went there.

Bill didn't know what to make of it. He didn't consider her his girl friend by any means; he had never so much as kissed her, or tried to, and it was always Emily who took his hand or put her arm through his, not the other way around. She was attractive, lively, intelligent, and apparently drawn to him, but yet he hesitated, puzzled by her. No girl had ever puzzled him that much before. But he had never know a girl quite like Emily before, either.

He realized that he was more than a little afraid of her.

She wasn't really part of his world. Her grandfather was a famous Senator; her family was active in politics, finance, commerce; she was rich, a bit spoiled, and very sure of herself. Even though she was two months younger than he was—Bill had checked that point out with Mel Salter—she seemed years older. She had been everywhere and done everything. He had gone once to Japan and once to Europe with his family; but Emily had been to Africa, Australia, Antarctica, South America, and any other continent worth naming, and last Christmas had spent her holiday on the Moon.

Bill had thought there was something brewing between Emily and Nick Antonelli. But Nick went to great pains to assure him that that was not the case. "We're old friends, is all. I dated her sometimes, Earthside. But she thinks I'm some kind of giraffe, and I think she's a merciless little shrew, and there isn't a whole lot of love between us. I still think you ought to marry her. She's definitely interested in you, and what's wrong with inheriting the Blackman millions?"

The idea of marrying anyone still struck Bill as grotesque, and of marrying Emily in particular as absurd. He tried to picture himself sitting down to dinner at the Blackman mansion and wondering which knife to use, how to make conversation with a Senator, what to say when they began talking high finance, and so on. He wouldn't fit in at all.

That was Mel Salter's theory of why Emily was acting this way, in fact. "It's an anthropological thing," he explained. "She doesn't know much about middle-class life. You're strange to her. Exotic. You grew up without servants. No robots in the house. Worry about college scholarships. You got to the Fair on brains, not pull. She wants to find out more about that kind of world."

It sounded convincing. Bill was not exactly charmed by the thought that Emily regarded him as a fascinating peasant whose mysterious middle-class customs were worthy of study. It made him all the more uncomfortable when he was with her to think that she might even now be making mental notes on his quaint habits of dress and speech. But the Emily mystery solved itself in late November, and it turned out that Mel's theory was wrong. Emily was after something quite specific and unsubtle.

He found out about it late one night as they were strolling through the amusement sector of the Fair. He had gone through a considerable chunk of that week's pay to take her on the gravity rides and into the horror house and down the row of international snack bars. They were walking arm in arm, and the gaudy colored lights of the amusement pavilions provided a hazy, dreamlike background, and suddenly they were in a dark place between two buildings and it seemed quite logical and appropriate to kiss her.

And afterward, when her lips pulled away from his and he stood there in an agreeably flustered way, he heard her whisper softly, "Bill, love, you know what I'd like to do now?"

"What?"

"Let's go up to the Mars Pavilion. Just the two of us—let's sneak in. I want you to take me into the dwelling chamber. I want to be right in there with the Martians!"

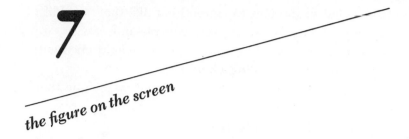

7

the figure on the screen

It was absolutely forbidden, of course. No one entered the dwelling chamber except staff researchers. Claude Regan himself would have to clear it with Dr. Martinson if he wanted to get in.

He explained that to Emily. Emily didn't care.

"I won't hurt them, silly! I just want to pick one of the Martian children up, maybe. And wander around their caves a bit. I've wanted to go in there ever since I first saw them. You'll help me do it, won't you, Bill? *Won't you?*"

Dismally, he began to understand. Emily had this crazy whim, and perhaps she had already tried to win admittance to the dwelling chamber and had been refused, and now she thought she could manipulate him into arranging things for her. So she had begun this curious romance. Did she really think he was so simple-minded? He could be thrown out of the Fair for something like that. A whiff of perfume, a kiss, softly spoken words—and was he supposed to be so goofy with love that he would obediently slip her into the dwelling chamber?

He said, "I can't do it, Emily. It's out of the question."

"Just for five minutes."

"Not for five seconds."

"You sound awfully stuffy when you talk like that," she said. She stood very close to him, the tips of her shoes pressing on his, her hands grasping his elbows, her body tilted far back so that he was supporting her. Her dark, shining eyes sparkled mischievously. In a soft, husky, coquettish voice she said, "Stop quoting rules at me and take me over there."

"No."

"As a very special favor?"

"No."

"As a very *very* special favor?"

"No."

"I won't hurt them. You can stay right next to me all the time. Who's going to notice?"

"The scientists," Bill said. "Probably two or three of them are working in the lab right now."

"That's downstairs. They won't pay any attention to what's going on above."

"There are big screens that show everything that takes place in the dwelling chamber."

"Well, we can wait a couple of hours, till they go to sleep," Emily suggested. "Then we can slip into the pavilion, and—"

"The pavilion is locked up tighter than a bank vault, Emily. I can't get inside it without two other members of the staff to help me finger the plates. And even if I could, I wouldn't do it."

"You don't like me," she pouted.

"That has nothing to do with—"

"It has everything to do with! If your girl from Earth came up here, I bet you'd take *her* in."

Bill let out his breath in a long burst of annoyance. "First thing is, I don't have a girl on Earth, not a regular one, anyway, and second thing is, if I did, I wouldn't violate the security of the Mars Pavilion for her, and third, why can't you just look through the glass like everybody else?"

"Because it's what everybody else does."

"And Emily Blackman has to be a special case?"

She made a face at him. "I want to touch them. I want to talk to them and hear them talk to me. I want them to know I'm there. Looking through glass isn't the same thing."

Pointing toward the nearby tower of a tridim palace, Bill said heavily, "If we move fast, we'll make the midnight show. They've got the Solar System premiere of the new—"

"You're changing the subject."

"Am I?"

"Bill, why are you so stubborn? I can't hurt the Martians, can I? I'll follow all your instructions. It's such a little little whim I have!"

"Which could cost me my little little neck," he said grimly. "For the last time, Emily, the answer is no, no, no, and No. Okay?"

She gave him a crafty smile. "Maybe we can make a deal."

"I don't want to hear—"

"You take me in to see the Martians, and I'll take you to see the Fair Satellite's missile defense system."

"The what?"

"I knew you didn't know about it! Come on. It'll shake you up plenty to see it. It's supposed to be top secret, but nothing stays secret up here very long. Come on!"

"Wait a second. I—"

But she had him by the wrist and was tugging him along with surprising strength. He nearly toppled at the first violent yank; then, willy-nilly, he found himself running along beside her. They sprinted through the wide midway of the amusement area, emerging on a ramp that led down to the lower levels of the Fair Satellite. Down, down, down, past the fifth overlevel, the fourth, the third, down to the main arcade, toward the Press Pavilion and on beyond it, into the shadowy corners of the structure. Emily ran easily, effortlessly, her glossy dark hair streaming out behind her. Bill loped along, keeping pace, feeling thoroughly out of control of events.

When she finally stopped running, they were in a part of the main arcade he had never seen before, back of the barracks-like rooms where visitors to the Fair were accommodated. Emily crouched and began to creep under an array of thick pipes that carried wastes from the buildings to the skin of the Satellite. "Careful," she warned. "Some of the pipes are hot, and I don't know which ones." He took care to keep well below any of them, which meant shuffling along almost on his knees.

After an endless crawl they came to an open area back of a vast hump that bulged out of the inner wall of the Satellite. Emily tapped the hump and said, "The main atmospheric recycler is housed in here. And just to the side of it, there ought to be a loose panel—ah—here it is—" She pressed both hands against the wall, and a metal panel that began at the level of her waist and was something less than one yard square swung aside. "Give us a boost," she said. "There—thanks. Now follow me."

He watched in amazement as she slithered into a small dark hole and vanished in the wall. Altogether against his better judgment, he pulled himself over the rim of the opening and shimmied inside.

"Leave the panel open," she called to him from somewhere far ahead. "Otherwise we may never find our way out!"

He could see nothing. The air in here was unpleasantly close and humid, and had a dank smell of lubricating oils and fuel. The passage was barely wide enough for him; the walls, when he touched them, were warm; and all about him came the throb and boom and hum of gigantic invisible machines. He crawled on and on and on, until at last a glimmer of light appeared in the blackness, and he saw Emily waiting for him ahead. The front of her short gray tunic was stained with grease. So were her hands, her knees, and her nose. There was a jagged tear in her tunic along the left hip. She was grinning.

"To our left," she said, "is the power unit for the atmospheric recycler. A little sand flung in the works would shortly create a remarkable stench throughout five levels. To our right is the recycler itself. A malicious person might consider the possibility of dumping a couple of pounds of pepper into it after signing up for the handkerchief concession. Straight ahead lies the outer skin of the Fair Satellite, and the missile-detection devices, all of which are fortunately aimed outward and so will fail to detect *us*."

"Who told you about all this?" Bill asked.

"It happens that I've been spending some time with a lovely boy on the security force," she said, with an arrogant, mocking little toss of her head. She spoiled the gesture by pushing her hair back from her forehead afterward, leaving another streak of grease. "We were looking for someplace really private," she added.

He ignored the thrust. Looking beyond her, he saw a narrow catwalk extending out over what seemed like a bottomless gulf. On the far side loomed a dark, coppery vault: the curving outer wall of the Fair Satellite. Emily led him across the catwalk, and as they spanned it he glimpsed a shelf at right angles to it, running right along the wall itself. Mounted just above that shelf—which was a ledge wide enough to hold several men—was an intricate array of complex instruments stretching off in both directions as far as he could see.

Emily said, "At this level there's a ring of infrared sensors going right around the Satellite. They can pick up the heat of a missile launching anywhere on Earth. One level up are trackers linked to the master computer; they deliver realtime calculations of the orbit of any object of visible mass heading in this direction. There's a second zone of sensors and trackers running around the Satellite from our north pole to our south pole; what you see here is our equatorial defense system. A couple of levels down are our counteroffensive missiles: tactical homing rockets with nuclear warheads. Those represent a last line of defense, since firing them might disturb the orbit of the Satellite. There are five little satellites in orbit around us, each armed with missiles of their own, and those will be

fired first in event of attack. The same spy satellites that
ran the video relays of the construction of the Fair are still
out there, helping to search for hostile missiles. Now, of
course, this whole system would break down if anything
happened to the master computer, and so—this is really
hush-hush, by the way—there's a *second* computer somewhere aboard, primed to take over in microseconds if the
main one goes. I'm not sure where it is, but I've got a
hunch that it's hidden on the staff level, maybe disguised
as kitchen equipment. If you lean forward, hanging on to
this railing, you can catch a peek at the inputs of our
survey antennae, which function all up and down the elec-
tromagnetic spectrum seeking approaching objects. Everything is arranged on a principle of triple or even quadruple
redundancy, so that several systems can be on the blink at
once and there'll still be an effective lookout kept. Of
course, you realize that there are other ways of blowing
up a space satellite like this besides aiming a rocket at it,
so that in a sense all this equipment gives only partial
security. For instance—"

"Hold it," Bill said, dazed by the smooth flow of her
recital. "Let me have a look at some of this stuff!"

"Look all you want," she told him. "We have plenty of
time."

He gripped the railing tightly and leaned forward, staring upward and downward in amazement.

Emily went on serenely, "For instance, as I was saying,
two or three really determined saboteurs could come here
containing the components of a small disassembled fission
bomb in their luggage. Each one carries a harmless quantity of fissionable material, say, but when they get together
they have critical mass. They could handle it as a suicide

mission, or perhaps could rig a timing device that would let them escape first. The security administrators are aware of this problem, and they've installed gamma detectors at many points on the Satellite to guard against this possibility, but even so—"

"I can't believe any of this," Bill cut in suddenly. "There's millions of dollars' worth of surveillance equipment here—maybe hundreds of millions! And you stand there talking about saboteurs with fissionables in their suitcases as though we're in immediate danger of being blown to pieces."

"We are," Emily said calmly.

"Those are just stories spread by people interested in making trouble for Claude Regan. Wild fables designed to keep attendance down."

"Do you think Regan would have spent this much to protect the Fair against wild fables?"

"Seriously, who would want to blow up the Fair? Aside from plain lunatics, who wouldn't have such an easy time getting hold of fissionable material in the first place."

"The Chinese, maybe. The Nigerians. Some nation that wants to see the United States finished as a world power. Bombing the Fair would not only cause billions of dollars in actual losses, it would hurt the prestige of the United States in—"

"That's nonsense," Bill said. "You can't really believe it. For one thing, nations don't blow each other up, any more. They have subtler ways of fighting. For another, a stupid act of aggression like that wouldn't damage our prestige, it would just hurt the insurance companies some, and—"

"Don't try to look at it rationally, Bill. I'm just giving you the irrational arguments. Killing and destroying are irrational acts. Claude Regan and Global Factors have plenty of irrational enemies who wouldn't be above an attempt on the Fair."

Bill considered the seething hatred that Regan inspired in Lou Pomerantz—a scientist, a man who in theory should be able to look at events coolly and objectively. He had to admit the possibility that in the world of business Regan might be hated far more violently even than that. Still, to destroy the Fair—

He felt a shiver of fear. He had never really taken the stories of possible danger seriously in the past, except for odd moments of fatigue-bred tension. But the sight of this fantastic collection of defense equipment was not particularly reassuring. Evidently the threat to the Fair was far from unreal, or a financially-pressed Regan would never have spent a fortune on sensors and anti-missile missiles.

He said, "How come you're still here, if you know all this?"

Emily laughed. "I like to live dangerously, don't you? Anyway, you can see that the Fair is taking precautions."

"But you just said—the men with the suitcases—"

"Oh, don't be such a worrier! If we go, we go, and meanwhile we're having fun. We ought to get out of here, now. One of the surveillance robots may come along and find us."

She led him back across the catwalk. As they started to crawl through the long grimy tunnel Bill said, "If the Fair is going to all this trouble to guard itself, how come anybody at all can get in here to inspect the defense system? Why aren't there scanners all over the place?"

"There are," Emily said. "They're out of order down this route, that's all."

"A decent computer would pick up the absence of a scanner signal, then."

"It would, except it's been programmed to overlook it."

"By whom?"

"The same security guards who unfastened that panel. They've rigged the whole thing so they can bring their girlfriends in here and wow them with a view of the defense setup."

"They can't be very seriously concerned about security matters, then."

"Oh, they aren't," Emily said. "They think it's all a big joke. Their minds work just the way yours does. They think nobody would possibly want to blow up the Fair, and that all the stuff we've just seen is a kind of decoration. And they're right, I suppose. Claude Regan put those sensors there so he could sleep better at night, but I can't get too excited about our chances of being blown up. You'd better not tell anybody about what I just showed you, though. Or bring anyone else in here."

"Why not?" Bill asked. "There's this cute little blonde usher at our pavilion that I was thinking of taking here, if—"

"Very funny." Emily didn't sound amused.

The wriggling journey to the exit from the wall was not as interminable as the inward crawl, but it took long enough. Seemingly hours later they came to the open panel; Emily slid through head first, doing a brief but adept handstand as she emerged, and Bill followed, not quite as gracefully. She put the panel back in place. There were streaks of grease all over her, now, and, looking down, he saw that he was in no better condition.

"Now you've seen it," Emily said. "Wasn't it fun?"

"Glorious. Like a sightseeing tour through a hospital."

"But it's comforting to know that all those sensors are watching for an attack," she persisted.

"And comforting to know that a clerk in the Press Pavilion can slither in there and sabotage the whole thing, if she gets into a sabotaging mood."

"That isn't so," Emily said. "I agree the security precautions are a little lax, but all sorts of alarms would have gone off if we had even touched one of those sensors. The boys on the patrol may be careless, but they aren't stupid. And you have grease an inch deep everywhere."

"So do you."

"It looks incriminating, doesn't it? But we can fix ourselves fast. In here."

She led him into a low, squat building near the place where they had entered the Satellite wall. Tools of all sorts were stacked on the floor. "It's the maintenance shack," Emily explained. "For the workmen who take care of the machinery behind the wall. And over here is a molecular bath that they use when it's time to clean up." She shut the door and stationed him beside it. "The door doesn't lock, so you'll have to stand guard. Nobody's likely to come prowling around here at this hour, but even so we don't want to take the chance, so lean against the door and make it seem locked to anybody who might try to come in." Her hands went to the magnetic catches of her tunic, and as she slipped out of the garment she added casually, "And keep your back turned. Peeking's no fair."

He pressed against the door and waited. In a moment he heard the hum of the molecular bath. Time ticked away slowly until finally Emily said, "All right. I'm decent."

Bill turned. She was more than decent: she was radiant, as shiningly clean as though she were on her way to her senior prom. She nodded toward the nozzle of the molecular bath. As he crossed the room to take his turn under it she said, "You really didn't peek!" She seemed surprised.

"How can you be so sure?"

"Because I was watching you all the time," she said.

He stood facing away from her, letting the ultrasonic waves go to work first on his bare skin and then on his grimy clothes, and wishing vaguely that he had never let himself get mixed up with Emily in the first place. She was too much for him. She made him feel like a big, bumbling fool most of the time. He didn't think he was a fool—just a bit naive and overearnest, maybe—but Emily set such a breathless pace with her pranks that he was forever tagging two paces behind, asking for explanations. He wished there was some way he could capture the initiative from her, some way of seeming less like a ninny and more like a hero when he was with her, but no ideas presented themselves.

He slipped back into his clothes and turned around. Emily was virtuously facing the door.

"Ready," he said.

Outside, she said, "Now you'll take me to visit your Martians."

"I thought we settled that issue a long time ago."

"I showed you the defense systems! You promised that you would take me to—"

"I never promised a thing," Bill yelled. "If you imagine we made a deal, you're 1000% wrong."

"You agreed to—"

114

"Beans. Listen, Emily, you asked me if I'd make a deal, and I said I wouldn't, and you started to run off somewhere, and I followed you, and the next thing I knew we were crawling through the walls, but that doesn't mean—"

He stopped. Tears were glistening in her eyes.

"You really did promise, you know," she said softly.

"That is absolutely not the case. And don't come on with the weeps, either, because I'm not impressed. If you want to be an actress, save it for the sensie scouts."

The tears vanished from her eyes as swiftly as they had sprouted. She glared at him.

"Let's just go over and look at the pavilion, then," she said. "You don't have to take me into the dwelling chamber if you don't want to."

"You figure you'll find a way of getting me to give in once we're there, don't you?"

"What's the harm of going over there?"

"It's late. Long after midnight. I go on duty at 0900 tomorrow morning."

"Baby needs his sleep. Mmmmm?"

"Besides," he went on sullenly, "there's always someone there to watch the environment dials, and if there are staff people there, you wouldn't stand a chance of having your way. So you may as well quit."

"Will you show me around the lab, at least?"

"You don't give up easily."

"It's a Blackman trait," she said. "We're a stubborn tribe. There was the year that all the polls said that Grandfather would lose the election, because he had voted to raise taxes when they needed money to pay for the space program, and he went out and campaigned anyway and won by a million votes. Why fight it, Bill? Take me over and show me around the lab."

Glumly he yielded, although not without telling himself that even if by some fluke he saw a way to slip her into the dwelling chamber, he would throw her bodily out of the pavilion before he allowed her to bamboozle him further. They found an upramp and headed for the fifth overlevel.

The Fair was a silent place. A few night-owl couples were strolling about, but hardly any Fairgoers were in sight; the pavilions closed at ten each evening, the luxury restaurants shut down two hours later, and at this time of night the only action was in the amusement area, on the far side of the Fair and four levels up. Though light gleamed everywhere, the corridors and pavilions had a forlorn, deserted, ghostly look.

They reached the Mars Pavilion and went around to the hidden staff entrance in back. It was useless to try the door, but he stood in the scanner field, activated the signal, and said, "Is anybody home in there?"

No answer. Shrugging, he turned to Emily and said, "See? We've had a long walk for nothing. Nobody's there, and my fingerprints alone won't get us inside, and I'm not going to start waking people up just so you—"

"You said someone has to be in there to watch dials," Emily reminded him.

The voice of Dr. Milbank said from within, "Is that you, Bill?"

"That's right, sir. I wonder if you could let me in. I— ah—have a friend with me."

"A moment," the scientist said.

He took more than a moment. But eventually the door slid open and the lean, myopic Milbank peered out, blinking uncertainly. He gave Bill a preoccupied smile, nodded distantly to Emily, and admitted them. "I've been running some tapes through the computer," Dr. Milbank said, as they descended to the laboratory level. "Just as we were closing to the public tonight, two of our little friends upstairs had some kind of dispute—the first quarrel we've ever observed among Martians. We taped the whole thing, naturally, and I've been trying to analyze it for content. I've come upon at least a dozen constellations of sound that I haven't heard before." Milbank chuckled ponderously. "Most of them not fit for polite company, I suppose. Heh-heh! Wouldn't it be interesting if we could decode Martian profanity? What could they possibly be profane about?"

Bill said, "Dr. Milbank, this is Emily Blackman. She's with the Press Pavilion, special assistant to Mr. Palisander. Dr. Milbank's a xenolinguist," he said to her.

Emily looked around the lab. "There doesn't seem to be anyone else here," she said.

"No, there isn't," said Dr. Milbank.

"But I remember that Bill explained to me that Dr. Martinson is the only one who can open the pavilion doors by himself. It seems that you have that privilege too."

"Someone could have come in with Dr. Milbank and then gone home," Bill said.

The xenolinguist nodded. "My assistant, Sid Webster, was with me until about an hour ago. Then he went to bed, and I stayed on alone. You see, Emily, it isn't necessary to have combinations of fingerprints to get *out* of the building, only when coming in. It's my shift to be watching the environment monitors, anyway, for the next hour and a quarter. That isn't really a job that requires full-time attention, so I've been putting in some after-hours work on these new tapes."

As Dr. Milbank spoke, Bill let his gaze roam idly toward the screens that relayed images from the dwelling chamber. He took a quick glimpse; and then, amazed, he looked again.

"Dr. Milbank, are you completely sure you were alone in the pavilion?" he asked.

"Of course. Why?"

"I thought I just saw somebody walk across the field of view on the dwelling-chamber screen."

"Impossible. No one's up there but the Martians."

"Out of the corner of my eye, though, I thought I had a quick view of—"

"You must have seen one of the Martians!" Dr. Milbank insisted.

"This was a human figure. A big one." Through Bill's mind raced Emily's lighthearted chatter about the enemies of Claude Regan who might want to blow up the Fair Satellite. There were other ways of making trouble for the Fair though. "It could be a saboteur," he said. "Trying to harm the Martians, maybe! I want to go up there and take a look!"

8

Everyone turned to look at the screens. All six of the Martians were visible, moving about in their slow, placid way. They gave no sign that an intruder might be among them, nor was any stranger in sight on the screens.

Bill wondered if his imagination might have been playing tricks on him. Worked up by Emily's talk of sabotage, annoyed by the ways in which she had made him seem foolish, eager somehow to look heroic and important before her—had he let himself invent that fleeting shape on the screen?

Then a large, shadowy, and undeniably human form came into view on the screen once again.

"There he is!" Bill said. "Look there!"

The figure stepped out of sight—but an elbow remained plainly visible for a long moment at the edge of the screen.

"I'll call the security forces," Dr. Milbank said.

"We can't wait that long," said Bill. "A stranger up there now—who knows what he's already done? I'm going up there to grab him!"

He started toward the spiral staircase leading from the lab to the dwelling chamber. Dr. Milbank called out to him not to go; Emily lunged at him, briefly catching his arm. He pulled free of her and rushed through the door. "Come back, Bill!" she cried. "Bill, be careful!"

He went speeding up the staircase and into the airlock at the top. Hurriedly he activated the airlock controls; it seemed to take a thousand years for the sixty-second recycling of atmospheres to be completed. As he waited he could picture the mysterious intruder lurching through the dwelling chamber, hurling the little Martians brutally against the cave walls, ripping the oxygen plants out by the roots, smashing, destroying, ruining. Wild with impatience, Bill hammered on the inner airlock door as though that could somehow get it to open more swiftly.

At last the airlock was free of its Earthside atmosphere. The thin, harsh air of the Martian cave came filtering in. Bill shivered. He had rushed up here without a thermal suit, without a breathing mask; suddenly he found himself plunged into temperatures barely above freezing and into air as thin as that on the highest mountains of Earth. His heart began to throb in wild thumps. His head started to pound. He sucked air through his mouth, hoping to take in more oxygen than his nostrils could supply.

It wasn't only the thinness of the air that was making his heart pound. He was unarmed and alone, and it now was occurring to him that heroism and foolishness were sometimes not so far apart. Whoever had broken into the pavilion must be dangerous, probably was carrying a weapon.

But there was no turning back now.

The airlock door opened on the dwelling-chamber side, and Bill stepped through, into the cave. One of the female Martians looked up at him in mild curiosity; the others did not pay any heed to his arrival. By the dim yellow glow of the luminous plants he counted three adults and one child. He could see the other child peering out shyly from one of the smaller rooms. Looking within, Bill saw the remaining adult squatting on a fiber mat against the far wall.

All of the Martians were safe, then.

Where was the prowler?

Bill stumbled from room to room, searching for the heavy-set man he had so fleetingly seen from below. There was no good hiding place in here—no closets, no alcoves, no nooks. Just the big room and the little ones, and it was impossible for anyone to get from one little one to another without going through the big room. By standing in the main chamber and circling around it from one little room to another, Bill knew, he should be able to find anyone hiding in here. But he saw no one.

He was growing dizzy. The thin air was getting to him. He swayed, sucked air deep into his lungs, coughed. He couldn't stay in here much longer. He was running short on oxygen; even he who had grown up in mile-high Denver couldn't adapt this quickly to so harsh an environment. If he didn't get out of here fast, he might collapse.

And the prowler?

The truth penetrated to Bill's oxygen-starved brain at last. The man hadn't been in the dwelling chamber! He must have been in the viewing chamber just outside the glass wall—the public section. Bill glanced in that direction, but of course could see nothing through the opaque wall of one-way glass. The scanner camera was not stopped by that glass, he realized; it must have looked right through, feeding the prowler's image to the screen and making it appear as though the man were actually in the dwelling chamber.

Bill shouted, "Dr. Milbank, can you hear me down there? He's not in with the Martians! He must be in one of the outer chambers! Are the security people here yet?"

"They're on their way," came Dr. Milbank's voice over the speaker.

"Send them in through the public entrance, one chamber at a time. Meanwhile I'll go into the viewing chamber and see if he's there."

"Bill, come down! Don't try to search for him!" It was Emily. "Please, Bill!"

Stubbornly he found the hidden panel opening into the airlock that connected the dwelling chamber to the public viewing chamber. He entered it, choking, gasping, slammed the hatch, got the pumps going. As good rich Earth air reached his lungs he closed his eyes, opened his mouth wide, and pulled the sweet stuff down. His head began to clear.

The door on the far side opened, and he edged cautiously into the viewing chamber.

The lights were off, and he had no idea how to turn them on. But his eyes had adjusted themselves to the dimness of the illumination in the cave of the Martians, and now just enough of their yellow glow was coming through the glass wall to allow him to see.

There was a man in a heavy overcoat at the far end of the viewing chamber, near the rear door.

He didn't look as big as he had seemed on the screen. The overcoat gave him extra bulk. Who would want to wear an overcoat on the Fair Satellite, Bill wondered, where the temperature was so carefully regulated for comfort? Bill couldn't see the man's face clearly, but it looked ugly, sinister, criminal. Was he hiding a load of bombs under that coat?

"All right, whoever you are," Bill said. "I see you. Put your hands up and turn your face to the wall!"

Instead of obeying, the stranger pulled back into the shadows until he was all but out of sight. Then he began to slink along the wall toward Bill.

Two can slink as well as one, Bill decided. He flattened himself against the opposite wall and crept silently along it toward the other man. As they drew close to one another the intruder seemed to go into a crouch, hands upraised and fingers spread as though about to pounce. Bill took the same position; and, like two wrestlers looking for an opening grip, they solemnly circled each other. The other man lunged; Bill sidestepped him; but it was only a feint, and the stranger pulled back quickly. Bill had his first clear look at the other's face: bloodshot eyes, yellowed teeth, skin lined with age.

He isn't armed, Bill thought, or he wouldn't be sneaking around like this. And he's a lot older than I am. I can take him. I can pin him fast and hold him until the security guards get here. If they ever bother to show up.

The lunge and feint had carried the intruder past Bill,

and now they moved along the other wall. The viewing chamber, like all the other chambers surrounding the core of the building, was circular, going completely around the pavilion, so they could stalk each other all year without ever reaching a dead end. They moved through the darkness, eyeing one another warily, neither making a break toward the other.

Now they were in front of the airlock panel leading to the dwelling chamber. Bill had revealed the position of the panel by emerging through it; and in their movements around the viewing chamber they had changed places so that the prowler was on the side of the wall where the panel was located. He whirled, suddenly, and tried to push the panel on its pivot and gain entry to the airlock.

But the panel could not be opened except by the right combination of authorized personnel. The intruder struggled with it; and Bill chose that moment to make his move. He leaped, caught the other man around the shoulders, and pulled him to the floor.

They rolled over and over. The prowler seemed hampered by his unwieldy coat, but he was surprisingly strong, and for an instant Bill felt himself pinned and helpless. He wedged one foot against the wall, though, pushed hard, and freed himself; and in the same motion he caught the intruder's collar and forced him face down against the floor. Bill got his knee into the small of the man's back and caught hold of an arm that was thrashing about wildly. The man grunted and kicked.

"Don't move or I'll break your back," Bill warned.

"Moron—idiot—assassin!" the prowler sputtered. "Release me! Vandal! Criminal!"

"Easy, now," Bill said. "Watch the language. And don't

try to move. Don't—try—to—*move.*"

He punctuated his words with jabs of his knee. The man continued to struggle for another moment, muttering thickly in what sounded to Bill like Russian or Polish. Then he got the message that Bill's knee was delivering to his back, and subsided.

Bill did not relax his grip. He held the man pinned face down for what felt like an endless length of time. At last the lights went on and people began rushing into the viewing chamber.

Dozens of security guards. Dr. Milbank. Lou Pomerantz, looking sleepy and worried. Sid Webster. Dr. Sullivan. One of the security men tapped Bill gently on the shoulder with the tip of an electric nerve-stunner and said, "Okay, you can get off him, son. If he tries anything I'll give him a jolt with the stunner."

Bill scrambled to his feet, blinking in the sudden brightness, and looked around for Emily. He didn't see her at all. It figures, he thought. I finally do something heroic and she doesn't even stay to watch.

The prowler got up slowly, brushing his trousers, scowling, talking to himself, straightening his back in a gingerly way. In the light he looked far less sinister: a short, rather beefy middle-aged man with dark rings under his eyes, puffy features, and a few strands of gray hair straggling across a bald dome. He pointed a hand shakily in Bill's direction and shouted, "Arrest him! He mugged me! Barbarian! Savage! Filth!"

"Dr. Magnitski!" Lou Pomerantz cried hoarsely.

He rushed to the stranger, who now was red-faced and close to apoplectic in his fury. Dr. Milbank gasped; Dr. Sullivan began to laugh; the security chief looked in bewilderment from one scientist to the next. Bill was mystified, but he began to get the uncomfortable sensation that a gigantic mistake had been made.

"Handcuff that criminal!" Dr. Magnitski was roaring. "He is a danger to society! He is an ape, a cretin, a Neanderthal! I demand that you imprison him for assault!"

The security chief said, "Would somebody mind explaining to me—"

"Dr. Magnitski is a leading Soviet authority on xenobiology," Lou Pomerantz said. "He—"

"Does that mean he's authorized to have access to this place at night?" the security man asked.

"Well, not exactly," Pomerantz said. "That is, he was invited here to examine our setup, but he wasn't due until next week. So I can't say what he's doing here now."

"And this kid here?" the security man asked, nodding at Bill.

"He is a criminal who assaulted me while I was doing scientific research!" Dr. Magnitski spluttered. "He must have broken in, thinking to do some harm here, and when he found me—"

"Hold it, doctor," said the security man. To Pomerantz he said, "Who is he?"

"He's on our staff," Pomerantz said. "I'll vouch for him."

The security man shook his head. "So who tackled who, and why? I heard there was a prowler in the pavilion. Which one of these two is the prowler—the Russian or the kid?"

Bill said, "No one was supposed to be up here on the main level at this hour. I was in the laboratory and saw this man's shape on our monitor screens, and came up to investigate. I found him wandering around. He wasn't anybody on our staff, and I didn't know anything about a Russian scientist supposed to be in here, so I told him to stand still and identify himself. Instead he jumped me. So—"

"I thought *he* was a prowler!" Dr. Magnitski roared. "And he—"

"And he—"

"And then—"

"The exit panel—"

"Brutal ruffian—"

"No explanation—"

"*Quiet, both of you!*" the security officer bellowed. He closed his eyes wearily for a moment. Then, turning to Magnitski, he said, "Doctor, would you mind telling us how you got inside the Mars Pavilion in the first place?"

"Very simple. I visited my good friend Dr. Martinson as soon as I arrived on this place. We talked in his office for a while. Then he invited me to go upstairs and view his Martians, which of course I was eager to do. The pavilion was closing, he said, and I would have the place to myself. He promised to join me in a few minutes. That was—oh, about the hour of 2230. Much time went by and Dr. Martinson did not appear. I discovered that I was locked in. It was strange, but I did not mind, because it gave me the opportunity to observe these fascinating beings in depth, and I assumed that in time Dr. Martinson would remember I was there and let me out. So I devoted several hours to my observations, and then suddenly this young brute slipped into the room and rudely ordered me to put up my hands. It was reasonable to believe that he was a criminal who intended harm to the pavilion, and so, although I am no longer a young man, I attempted to apprehend him, but his strength prevailed, and—"

"Thank you, Dr. Magnitski," the security man cut in. He said to an aide, "Find Martinson and let's hear his version."

As though on cue, Dr. Martinson burst into the room. He looked more haggard and wild-eyed than ever, and seemed appalled at the quantity of strangers in the pavilion at this hour. "My God!" he cried. "Dr. Magnitski! I completely forgot about you!"

The Russian managed a heavy laugh. "Which has caused a great deal of excitement, it seems," he said.

The security man stepped forward. "Dr. Martinson, there's been some confusion here, but I think you can clear it up in a hurry. This man claims to be a Soviet scientist, and—"

"Yes, of course. He's my valued colleague Roman Magnitski, of the University of Odessa," Dr. Martinson said. "He got here this evening—a little ahead of schedule; the computer seems to be mixing things up again—and unfortunately I was called away to a late meeting and left him here without notifying my staff of his arrival, and the meeting was unexpectedly long, and—"

Bill sank into deep gloom as the explanations unfolded. It was altogether clear to him now that he had done something marvelously idiotic, though it had not entirely been his fault. There *had* been an unexplained prowler in the pavilion, after all, and how was he supposed to guess that he was tackling a famous scientist who had Dr. Martinson's permission to be there?

The misunderstanding was patched up without further difficulty. The Russian, Dr. Martinson declared, would have free access to the pavilion for the duration of his visit; and after apologizing profusely for having left his guest stranded for hours in the locked pavilion, Dr. Martinson insisted that Bill and Dr. Magnitski conclude their hostilities with a handshake.

The Russian still looked disgruntled, and Bill felt so sheepish about the whole thing that he could barely look the other man in his bloodshot eyes. But they shook, finally, and Bill murmured something apologetic. "It wouldn't have happened," Bill couldn't resist adding, "if you had told me who you were."

"I took you for a criminal," said the Russian stiffly. "I do not introduce myself to criminals!" And he walked away, still looking very much ruffled, while Dr. Martinson attempted to soothe him.

The security men left the pavilion, as did the xenobiologists who had been awakened by Dr. Milbank. Bill thought about going off somewhere to hide for a while. Turning, he peered through the glass wall into the dwelling chamber and saw a slim figure clad in breathing mask and thermal suit in the main part of the cave, cuddling one of the Martian children. It was no great challenge to guess the masked one's identity.

Emily.

Bill went down the back stairs to the laboratory, put on a breathing mask himself, and cycled through the airlock into the dwelling chamber. Emily was trying to teach the little Martian to clap hands, now, but the alien child did not seem eager to learn.

"All the excitement over?" she asked. "I hear you caught the dangerous prowler and he turned out not to be so dangerous."

He forced himself to ignore her mocking words. "How

did you get in here?" he shouted.

"Not so loud!"

"How did you get in here?"

"Through the airlock, silly. How else?"

"But you aren't supposed to—authorized personnel only—the regulations—"

"While you were playing policeman," Emily said, "Dr. Milbank asked me to go up into the dwelling chamber and make sure that everything was really all right. He wasn't worried one bit about the regulations. He showed me how to use the breathing mask and put me through the airlock."

"So you managed to get in here after all," Bill said darkly.

"Thanks to you, sweet! If you hadn't touched off that little crisis with the Russian, I would never have set foot in here." She came toward him and gave him a sisterly little kiss on the cheek. "You were wonderful, Bill," she murmured. "So very brave. And even if you didn't mean to, you let me have my visit with the Martians. I can't begin to tell you how grateful I am."

He wasn't sure how seriously to take her words. There was no mistaking the gleam of triumph in her eyes, though. She had had her way. As usual. As always. She was just too much.

He said hoarsely, "If you don't mind, I think I'll call it a night. Can I show you to your dorm?"

They left the pavilion and hurried downramp to the staff quarters. Outside her dormitory she took his hand briefly.

"Poor Bill," she said. "I must have given you a terrible time tonight. I'm so sorry. Thanks for everything, love.

And sleep well, won't you?"

"Somehow I doubt that I will," he muttered, and headed for his room.

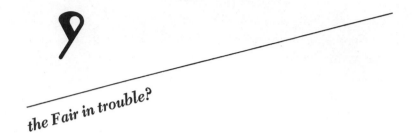

9
the Fair in trouble?

The Soviet xenobiologist spent a week at the Fair, nearly all of it at the Mars Pavilion. He asked endless questions, examined everything, hardly ever set foot in any other part of the Fair. Then he went away.

Bill was glad to see him go, since Magnitski had never forgiven him for the circumstances of their first meeting, and stared at him coldly whenever they happened to meet in the laboratory. It was a pity, Bill thought, that they had had such a bad introduction to each other, since the Russian was probably a decent enough sort; he went out of his way to invite the pavilion scientists to visit the zones where the Russians were doing research on Mars. And it was important, Bill knew, that there be a free flow of scientific information among nations. Yet as long as Magnitski was around the place, Bill felt uncomfortable.

Once the visitor was gone, Bill slipped back into his normal routine. He was mixed up in half a dozen research projects at once, running breathlessly from Lou Pomerantz' part of the lab to Dr. Milbank's, and from Dr. Milbank's to Dr. Sullivan's, and so on to the point of near-exhaustion. He loved every hectic moment.

He was more than just an errand boy or mascot around the lab now. The xenobiologists had discovered that Bill could be useful in more important ways. He had a solid knowledge of their field, especially for someone who hadn't even been to college yet, and he rapidly grasped details of their current work. Also he had one of the most valuable gifts a scientist could have: the knack of making inspired guesses. From a few seemingly unrelated scraps of data he could put together a working theory that often served to lead the way into a fruitful field of investigation. (Just as often his theory turned out to be altogether wrong—but that didn't matter. Negative conclusions could sometimes be as useful as positive ones. What counted was his ability to suggest a logical next step.)

Bill found himself spending a good deal of time inside the Old Martians' dwelling chamber. More and more of the research depended on actual contact with them, instead of on remote telemetering of information; and the Martians appeared to be much more tolerant of the presence of Earthmen in their chamber now than when they first had arrived. They even were willing to put up with a certain amount of direct physical examination.

There were various theories to account for this change in their attitude. Dr. Sullivan thought it was because they had been separated from their own kind on Mars for so many months that they were becoming more sociable than

Martians normally were. They were mellowing, she said, and starting to look upon the scientists as friends.

Lou Pomerantz had an entirely different view. He maintained that the Martians' spirits had been broken by what amounted to forced confinement, and that they simply did not care what happened to them now. Their new "friendliness" was a sign of inner collapse.

Bill's own opinion zigzagged between the two ideas. Certainly the Martians seemed like forlorn, hopeless, pathetic creatures. They spent hours staring at the emptiness before them; they wandered aimlessly around their chamber; they said little to each other and almost nothing to the Earthmen. Ripped from their own civilization—itself dying and pitiful—they seemed much of the time like helpless waifs condemned to an imprisonment they could not begin to understand.

But at other times he thought he could see beyond the dismal surface to the strength beneath. It was a mistake, he told himself, to think that the Martians were pathetic simply because Nature had given them big wobbly heads, sad-looking eyes, and small scrawny bodies. The impression of misery that they gave was not necessarily a reflection of their true inner selves. These were people of an old, tough, durable race who had survived thousands upon thousands of years in a savagely hostile environment. It was wrong to get too sentimental about them when one had little idea of what was really going on in their minds.

As he spent more time in their company, he was less and less inclined to regard them as unhappy victims of fate. They were solemn and reserved, yes, but they could also be amiable, friendly, even affectionate. He detected individual personalities in them. The bigger male, who spoke the most English and seemed to be in charge of the whole group, was self-assured and calm; his companion tended to be a little jittery, and was uneasy about submitting to any kind of examination. One of the females was almost lively, as Martians went, with a bold, playful, teasing nature; the other was shy and easily upset. The two children seemed curious, unafraid, and alert.

The Martians had no names, as far as anyone could tell; they did not even seem to comprehend what it meant to have a name, despite Dr. Milbank's long explanations of the concept. Officially they were known in the laboratory simply as Male-One, Male-Two, Female-One, Female-Two, Male-child, and Female-child. But as Bill got to know them better he privately renamed them Moe and Joe, May and Fay, Jack and Jill, and when some of the researchers heard him using the names, they adopted them also. It was amazing how much more like a person a Martian could seem if you called him "Moe" instead of "Male-One." Only Dr. Sullivan rejected the scheme and went on using the more dignified names for the Martians.

The weeks went along. It was late December, now; the Fair was into its third month. Bill was so preoccupied with his work at the pavilion that he paid scarcely any heed to outside events. He dimly remembered that there was a place called Earth, 50,000 miles away; once a month he dutifully phoned his parents and smiled to them across the gulf of space, and listened to his kid brother's chatter about the basketball season, and heard his sister talk about her approaching wedding. When he called at Thanksgiving time, there was some discussion about whether he would come home for Christmas, when his sister was getting married. They went round and round on it for five very expensive minutes before Bill finally figured out what the trouble was.

His mother, who could be old-fashioned in some ways, thought that it would be proper for him to be there for the ceremony. But at the same time she regarded space-flight as horribly unsafe, and didn't want him to make any more trips than absolutely necessary. She was so completely split between the two opposing desires that she had the whole family in confusion. In the end Bill had to solve the problem himself. He would not make the trip to Earth for the wedding, but they would hook up a space-relay telephone call so he could watch the most important part of the ceremony and congratulate the bride.

His sister seemed satisfied by that. She would be seeing him soon enough, anyway, she said, because she and her bridegroom were going to spend a week of their honeymoon at the World's Fair in early January.

"Great!" Bill said. "And what about the rest of you? When are you coming up here?"

His father looked uneasy. His mother's jaws clamped in a way that announced family disagreement. After a long, uncomfortable pause, his father said, "We're still trying to work it into the schedule, Bill. We haven't decided the date yet."

"It's a great show, Dad. If you wait too long you may not be able to get reservations at all."

"Don't worry about us. We'll be up there one of these days, Son."

From his father's tone of voice and his mother's expression Bill suspected that they wouldn't be. Given his mother's attitude toward spaceflight, that wasn't greatly surprising.

When he talked to the family again just before Christmas, he learned that even his sister wasn't coming. "We're honeymooning in Antarctica instead," she told him. "It's supposed to be beautiful there in midsummer—we'll go skiing and visit the penguins and—"

"You can see penguins in the zoo," Bill said in annoyance. "We've got *Martians* here. Why did you change your plans?"

"Oh, things came up," she said hazily, and changed the subject.

That bothered him. It bothered him enough so that he asked her about it again a few days later on her wedding day. He watched the ceremony on the telephone screen, thinking that he had never seen his sister look more beautiful than in her shimmering white gown; and afterward, when she came to the phone to receive his congratulations, he said, "I still wish you were coming here next week, the way you planned."

He saw her exchange glances with her groom.

She said, "Don't start that now, Bill."

"When will you come to the Fair, then?"

It did not occur to him just then that the cancellation of his sister's trip to the Fair, and the reluctance of his mother to go there, might be part of some larger pattern. It did not even occur to him that the Fair was any less crowded in January than it had been in October. There always seemed to be a long line in front of the Mars Pavilion; and he was much too busy to follow daily news events. So it hit him hard one night soon after the turn of the new year when Mel Salter said, "Well, looks like we'll all be going home soon."

"What do you mean?" Bill asked.

"Fair's closing down. Got the word from Emily. They'll try to keep it open till April 12, make it an even six months. Then that's the end."

"*What?* Are you joking, Mel? Why should the Fair close?"

"Money. Shortage thereof. Haven't you been watching the attendance figures?"

Bill turned in bewilderment to Nick Antonelli. "The place is mobbed every day, isn't it? What's he talking about?"

"Attendance is down 50% from the average of the first week," Antonelli said. "And going down from one week to the next. You mean you haven't noticed?"

"I thought the Fair was a sellout," Bill said. "On account of the Martians—booked solid for months—"

"It was." Antonelli shrugged. "Then the cancellations started, along about the third week. I understand there's practically no advanced sale past February, now. They're running cut-rate specials on transportation and accommodations, and still nobody wants to come up here. Your own sister cancelled out, didn't she? She wasn't the only one."

"But why?"

"Same story as before," said Nick. "Talk of sabotage. Rumors that ships coming to the Fair will be blown up in space, or that the whole Fair will be bombed. All sorts of wild things are circulating Earthside. The general opinion is that the Chinese are going to do it."

"That's lunacy," Bill muttered. "Neither the Chinese nor anybody else has any motive for harming the Fair. Only a sick mind would believe stories like that."

"You don't have to be sick to believe them," Nick said.

"Just easily scared. The majority of the people on Earth who could afford to come to this Fair are easily scared. They have things pretty good in life, and they don't want to take any risks just for the sake of having a little fun in space. So all the cautious ones are cancelling their trips. Before long some worried parents are going to be ordering their children home from here, too. My guess is that the Fair won't last another month. The overhead is too high. The place is losing millions every week."

"But can't Regan convince the public that there's no danger of sabotage? I mean, he's got this fantastic collection of defensive devices in the skin of the Satellite, and—"

Bill stopped, realizing he wasn't supposed to know anything about those defensive devices.

Nick and Mel smiled. Mel said, "Bet I know where you found out about those!"

Bill kept a shamefaced silence.

Nick said, "Bet I know too. Emily took you on the tour, eh?"

"Well—"

"Come on. You're among friends. Anyway, those things aren't going to be secret much longer. Regan's calling a press conference for early next week and he's going to take everybody on a tour of the defense installations. Every network will run shots of them."

"How do you know that?"

"Emily told me," Nick said. "It's being arranged through her office, naturally."

"Won't work," said Mel. "Only scare people more. Show 'em all that stuff, they'll decide there must be a real danger somewhere. Fair's going to close."

"It can't!" Bill said. "I mean—well, what would they do with everything? The Satellite—the pavilions—?"

"No problem," Nick told him. "The way I hear it, Regan's going to sell the place to a group of corporations that'll run it as a kind of space resort. Meeting halls for conventions, exhibits, things like that. Since he won't be involved with it, and it won't be any kind of national project, it's thought that there won't be any danger of bombing. The pavilions will be cleaned out. Your Martians will get home to Mars a few months early, I guess. And we'll all get home to Earth."

Bill was stunned. They were just beginning to make some progress with the Old Martians now. Dismantling the lab at this point would be a monstrous scientific mistake; there was no way to duplicate on Mars the research facilities that they had here, and the interruption in the work would set xenobiology back a long way.

Besides, he was entitled to a full year at the World's Fair. It seemed like a cruel joke of fate to snatch him away so soon from the biggest experience of his life.

Nick and Mel appeared to take a lighter outlook. To them the Fair was a lark, an interlude in more serious matters. They were both disappointed at the prospect that the holiday might be ending ahead of time, but clearly they did not view the Fair's failure as any kind of personal catastrophe.

Now that it had been called to his attention, Bill could see that the Fair definitely was languishing. He checked the daily attendance figures; they were down sharply from the opening weeks, and continued to decline almost in a straight line from day to day. There were vacancies in the Fair's hotels. The crowds around the Mars Pavilion and the neighboring Hall of the Worlds were misleading, for those were by far the most popular pavilions, and everyone who did come to the Fair made sure to see them more than once. But in his off hours Bill wandered to some other sections of the show and saw the difference. The Telephone Pavilion, where electronic marvels had attracted thousands a day, had no waiting line at all now. Ushers were standing in front of the Global Factors Pavilion inviting passersby to step inside. It was the same everywhere else. A few pavilions were totally deserted. Restaurants were doing poor business. A mood of despair seemed to be spreading through every part of the Satellite. It amazed Bill that he had noticed none of this before.

But there was no official announcement that the Fair might be closing. The big bulletin board outside the Press Pavilion continued to list special events on into September. Was it only a pretense, Bill wondered, for the sake of keeping up appearances? Or had the rumors of a closing been greatly exaggerated, and was the Fair going to stick it out despite the heavy losses?

He tried to get some information out of Emily. But she was slippery and evasive.

"I haven't seen any announcement of a closing," she said.

"Of course not. There hasn't been one. What I want to know is if they've made a decision to shut the place down."

"Why don't you ask Claude Regan, Bill?"

"Very amusing. Look, Emily, any kind of news like that is bound to cross Mr. Palisander's desk, and what crosses his desk crosses yours, so—"

"As far as I know," she said, "the Fair is going to remain open as scheduled."

Her eyes twinkled playfully at him, contradicting her words. She was as exasperating as ever. He felt like accusing her of deliberately hiding the truth from him. He wanted to let her know that Nick Antonelli and Mel Salter had admitted learning about the closing from her. But what good would it do? She would simply deny everything. In despair he gave up.

He lived in dread, now, of an official closing announcement. But the days passed and lengthened into weeks, and nothing was said about an impending end to the Fair. Attendance even picked up a little in mid-January; the word was that Regan had launched an extra-heavy promotion campaign on Earth. It was still terribly quiet in many parts of the Fair, and even in the dormitories, for a number of Fair employees were leaving. Some were simply laid off because there was nothing for them to do, or let go as economy moves. Others were pulled home by anxious parents who were convinced that the Fair Satellite might be destroyed by villainous saboteurs at any time. When he talked to his parents in January, Bill realized that they were searching for some way to tell him to come home. They couldn't come right out and say it in that many words, for they knew how hard he had worked to get this opportunity, and how much it meant to him to be at work in the Mars Pavilion. But they looked drawn and tense, as if they spent most of their time worrying about him.

His mother said, "Don't you think you've had about enough of the World's Fair by now? Four months with your Martians ought to be plenty, I'd say."

"You know that isn't true, Mom. They're only just starting to trust us now."

"Your father and I think you should be spending some

time getting ready for college, too. It'll probably take months for you to buy everything you'll need, and—"

"It shouldn't take more than about three days," Bill said. "And college is a long way off, anyhow."

Bill couldn't blame her for being edgy, considering some of the stories that must be going around down there; but he wasn't going to let malicious rumors do him out of an experience like this. No doubt the Fair did have enemies—or Claude Regan did, at any rate—but they weren't really likely to do anything murderous. They were managing quite nicely to damage Regan's bank account simply by spreading rumors. And the Fair had been running for months, now. If someone planned to blow it up, why wait this long? So Bill calmed his mother as well as he could, and sidestepped her attempts to get him to leave.

Despite such things—and the air of general dismay and foreboding that seemed to hang over the entire Fair—Bill managed to push out of his mind the possibility that it all might soon come to an end. Especially when he was working at the Mars Pavilion, deeply absorbed in the problems of Martian metabolism or Martian linguistics or Martian psychology, it was easy to shut out all unpleasant thoughts and dwell only on the challenges at hand.

Bill was in the laboratory one morning early in February when the bulky figure of Roger Fancourt appeared with Dr. Chiang. The news commentator had visited the lab in October, while he was doing his general coverage of the entire Fair, but Bill hadn't seen him since. He wasn't even sure that Fancourt would remember who he was; the only time they had spoken was when they had had adjoining cradles on the shuttle ship from Earth, and that seemed like millions of years ago.

Fancourt smiled genially at Bill, who was processing some of Dr. Milbank's latest language tapes, and said, "Good morning, Bill. How's everything going?"

"We're keeping busy," Bill said, getting to his feet. "I guess you're here to see Dr. Martinson, eh? Let me buzz his office and I'll find out if—"

"No, I don't want to see Martinson," Fancourt said. "I'd like to talk to you, though."

"Me?"

"Bill Hastings of Denver, Colorado. That's who I'm looking for. There isn't anybody else around this pavilion named Bill Hastings, is there?"

"Well, no, but—"

"Can I have about half an hour with you, then? You remember, when we rode up here together, you promised that you'd fill me in some day about your Pluto theories. We never did get a chance to discuss them on the flight. But now I'm back for a second look around the Fair, and I though I'd keep my date with you. Okay? If it's not convenient for you to talk with me now, we can set up something for this afternoon, or tomorrow, or whenever."

"You aren't joking? You really want to know about—"

"The whole scoop, Bill. As I say, if it isn't convenient now—"

"Oh, no," Bill said, getting over his astonishment. "That is, I suppose what I'm doing can wait a little while. I can always make up the time later. Sure."

"Not here," Fancourt said. "At the Press Pavilion."

"Nobody'll mind if we talk here. If we go into one of the side offices, we won't be disturbing anyone, and—"

"But my videotaping facilities are at the Press Pavilion, Bill. Everything's all set up for the interview over there."

"You want to tape this?" Bill asked.

"You bet. An interview isn't an interview unless it's on tape. Ready to go over?"

"I suppose I am," Bill said. He was thoroughly baffled by Fancourt's sudden interest in him. But the big newsman offered no explanations as they left the Mars Pavilion and headed toward the press headquarters.

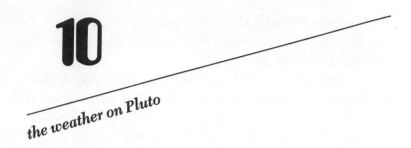

10

the weather on Pluto

The Press Pavilion seemed extraordinarily busy. Recently, when Bill had stopped in there to say hello to Emily, he had been struck by how quiet the place was; only a skeleton corps of newsmen seemed to be covering the Fair, now that the excitement of the first few weeks had passed. But today the place was full of journalists, in the lounges, at the computer outputs, and everywhere else. Something unusual was very obviously about to happen, Bill realized. He hoped it wasn't going to be an announcement that the Fair was closing ahead of schedule.

Roger Fancourt steered him through the crowd. Emily appeared from one of the inner offices and gave Bill an odd, smirking, I-know-something-you-don't-know sort of smile.

"Everything's ready, Mr. Fancourt," she said. "If you'll

both come this way—"

She led them to one of the video studios on the second floor of the pavilion and left. Fancourt indicated that Bill should take a seat at a low table in the middle of the room. Along one wall was a glass panel leading into a control room. The snout of a television camera jutted from the ceiling.

Fancourt said. "Before we actually begin, Bill, let's talk a little for test purposes. You've been interviewed for video before, haven't you?"

"Yes, sir. After I won the essay contest."

"Then you know something of what we want. Just keep your head up—don't need to look at the camera all the time—get the voice a little stronger—let's hear you say something, now."

"May I ask a question, Mr. Fancourt?"

"Of course."

"Why are you interviewing me?"

"You're the winner of an important nationwide contest," Fancourt said.

"That's old stuff. Last summer's news."

"But you have some interesting ideas that haven't been discussed on my program." Fancourt reached into a brief-case and pulled forth a sheaf of papers. He showed the top page to Bill, who saw the familiar opening words of his own essay on Life on Other Worlds. "I'm interested in your ideas on Pluto, Bill. We may be doing a little feature on the unexplored regions of the Solar System, and I'm lining up some advance material. I've read your essay, and what I understand of it is very exciting. I just want you to explain it in simple terms."

"The whole essay, or just the Pluto part?"

"Just the Pluto part. You'll see what I want when I lead into the introduction. Be as technical as you like, but remember that the people who'll be watching you aren't scientists, and don't know what you mean, by, ah—super-conductivity, say, or superfluidity. Or absolute zero, even."

From the control room came a technician's voice: "All set, Mr. Fancourt."

The studio lights grew brighter. A red light came on. Fancourt said easily and smoothly, in that deep-voiced delivery that so many millions of viewers knew so well, "Ladies and gentlemen, I'm talking tonight with Bill Hastings, a native of Denver who's been hailed by space scientists as America's most farsighted young man. Bill's gaze is focussed way out—on the cold and distant planet of Pluto, in fact. Last year his essay on Life on Other Worlds brought him top honors in a contest involving a million and a half high school seniors. Bill, would you tell us about the prize you won?"

"I was granted a year at the Mars Pavilion of the World's Fair," Bill said. "Working with the scientists who are studying the six Old Martians living there."

"And that's where I'm talking with Bill Hastings right now, ladies and gentlemen—50,000 miles out in orbit, at the Columbian Exposition itself. How are the Martians doing, Bill?"

"Real well. They were pretty aloof at first, but now they're cooperating nicely with us, and we're learning a great deal about their—"

"Fine," Fancourt said abruptly. "Getting on to the subject of your prize-winning essay, now: the part that attracted the attention of space experts, I understand, is where you speculate on the forms of life that we might expect to find on Pluto. Let's talk about Pluto a while, shall we? It's the outermost planet of the Solar System, of course, and—"

"Actually it isn't," Bill said. "Not at the moment, anyway."

Fancourt looked mystified. "It isn't?"

"Pluto's a strange planet with a very strange, elongated orbit. The orbit's extremely eccentric—that is, it's flattened, rather than being almost a circle, as the orbits of the other planets are—and as a result Pluto's orbit overlaps the orbit of Neptune. It takes Pluto 248 of our years to make one complete orbital trip around the Sun, and most of that time Pluto stays outside Neptune's orbit, but it does cross it some of the time. About thirty years ago Pluto came across Neptune's orbit on the way in, and since 1989 Pluto has been constantly closer to the Sun than Neptune. But Pluto will start moving outward again. On the average it's almost a billion miles farther from the Sun than Neptune—3700 million miles to 2800 million miles. Only not now."

Fancourt frowned. "Does that mean there's a danger of a collision between Neptune and Pluto some year when they cross orbits?"

"Oh, no," Bill said. "The orbits are always crossed. An orbit is just an imaginary line through space, you know. What counts is the position of the planet *along* its orbit, and whenever Pluto crosses Neptune's orbit, Neptune is always somewhere else, far away along its own orbit. The Solar System couldn't work any other way. The laws of celestial mechanics—"

"We seem to be getting a little off our own orbit," Fancourt said. "Regardless of Pluto's—ah—unusual orbit, it's correct to say that Pluto is an immense distance from the Sun, eh, Bill? And therefore what kind of planet can we expect it to be?"

"A miserably cold one. The Sun is so far away that it'll seem like just another star. Without solar heat, the surface temperature on Pluto will be close to absolute zero—the lowest temperature that can possibly be attained in the universe."

"How much colder is absolute zero than, well, ordinary zero?"

Bill grinned. "On the Centigrade scale, absolute zero is about —273°. In Fahrenheit terms it's—let's see—" He paused. He wasn't used to thinking in the old-fashioned Fahrenheit system, which was no longer officially in use anywhere, but he knew that the older members of Fancourt's audience still clung to it. "Absolute zero in Fahrenheit is about —460°. I could work it out more exactly if—"

"No need. We can tell it must be plenty cold!"

"The entire planet is frozen," Bill went on. "What would be liquid on Earth is solid there. Elements that are gases here could exist only in liquid form there. If there's any atmosphere, it would consist of just the lightest elements—hydrogen, helium, maybe neon. No oxygen, no nitrogen, nothing we could possibly breathe—those gases would have to be liquid at such temperatures. Pluto must be one huge field of ice, perhaps with seas of liquid methane."

"Your essay, Bill, claims that life can exist on a planet like that. Seems to me that's a little far-fetched."

"Obviously life as we know it can't have evolved there," Bill said. "By which I mean protoplasmic oxygen-breathing life based on a carbon chemistry. Our sort of life doesn't tolerate a very wide temperature range and can't survive in the absence of water or oxygen, so it's out as far as Pluto's concerned—or as far as any of the other planets of the Solar System are concerned, except Mars, where a suitable environment is maintained only in caves. But that doesn't mean we can rule out other forms of life."

"How would you define life, anyway?" Fancourt said.

Bill smiled. "We could go around and around on that one all night. No matter what definition I give, somebody could always find some borderline case that doesn't quite fit—like the viruses. But I'll take the risk. At the very minimum, a living creature carries on continuous energy-producing chemical reactions and is able to sustain those reactions as long as a supply of fuel is available to it. A living creature should be able to duplicate itself—that is, to reproduce. It should remain chemically stable under whatever are normal conditions for its existence."

"That sounds good enough to me," Fancourt said.

"It really isn't, though. With the right sort of twisting of ideas you could prove that the flame of a candle is 'alive,' using those definitions. But it's a place to begin." Bill leaned forward, spreading his hands wide as though trying to seize and possess the concepts he knew so well. "Now: for life, a basic substance is needed, a building-block material that readily forms complex chemical compounds. On Earth that basic substance is carbon. Next, a solvent is necessary—a substance in which the chemical reactions of life take place. The solvent for life as we know it is water—which limits the range of our kind of life generally to the zone between 0° and 100°C., freezing and boiling. Finally, there has to be some form of chemical reaction that produces the energy needed to sustain life. There are various reactive systems, but the one that works here involves oxygen, which combines with other elements to yield heat."

Fancourt said, "Aren't there certain bacteria that get along without oxygen at all?"

"The anaerobic bacteria, yes," Bill said. "They don't draw oxygen from the atmosphere, but they need it all the same. They obtain their oxygen chemically, from the breakdown of oxygen-containing compounds."

"Then there can't be any life-form that doesn't make use of oxygen in one way or another?"

"Not on Earth. But we can imagine some wholly alien' life-forms. Say, one based on silicon instead of carbon. Silicon has many of the same chemical properties as carbon. Living things can obtain energy in other ways than through oxygen reactions, too. We can dispense with oxygen and water altogether and surround our supposed critter with liquid ammonia or liquid methane, both of which are abundant on every planet from Jupiter outward."

"But the combination of elements that we call protoplasm," Fancourt said. "If you eliminate them, is there really anything left that we can recognize as life?"

"If it reacts chemically with its environment to obtain energy, and if it reproduces, we can say that it's alive. Even if it isn't protoplasmic. For example, on Pluto—"

"Yes," said Fancourt eagerly. "On Pluto."

"Because of the extremely low temperature, there can't be any atmospheric oxygen, nor can H_2O exist in the liquid form. That rules out our kind of life. But what I've described in my essay is a crystalline life-form existing close to absolute zero, made up mainly of cobalt and silicon, needing very little in the way of energy to stay alive, and possibly even intelligent, carrrying on its thought processes by virtue of superconductivity, and—"

"Wait a while!" Fancourt said. "You're moving much too fast for me, Bill. A crystalline life-form?"

"Yes. To us it would look lifeless, I suppose. But on its own terms it would be alive—and durable enough, because of its crystalline structure, to stand up to conditions on Pluto, where the weather isn't very pleasant."

"Why cobalt and silicon?"

"Silicon, as I've explained, is a suitable basic element for a non-protoplasmic life-form, because of its chemical properties. Cobalt is a fairly scarce metal which we use in magnets, electronic devices, and as a blue pigment. When silicon and cobalt combine in a cubic crystal structure they become a superconductor, even though by itself cobalt isn't superconductive and silicon, which isn't a metal, isn't even an electrical conductor."

"Tell us a little about superconductivity," Fancourt prompted, glancing at an open page of Bill's essay.

Bill drew a deep breath. "It's a phenomenon that was discovered at the beginning of the twentieth century by a Dutch physicist. He put an electric current through some frozen mercury and found that at a few degrees above absolute zero all resistance to the flow of the current disappeared. You know, ordinarily when you pass a current through a conductive substance, the electrons of the current collide with the vibrating atoms making up the crystal structure of the conductor. The result is what we call resistance—the current has to fight its way through. The higher the temperature, the wider is the area of vibration of the atoms in the crystals, and the greater the number of collisions—so resistance rises with temperature. Down around absolute zero there's no resistance at all—a current sent through a superconductor will flow just about forever without encountering friction. If we put a current into a ring of superconductive metal, it'll persist indefinitely."

"Isn't that a kind of perpetual motion?" Fancourt asked. "I thought perpetual motion was impossible."

Bill shrugged. "If you consider the persistence of an initial current without any further input of energy to be perpetual motion, well, the superconductive ring is giving you perpetual motion. And of course people have been searching for centuries for some sort of machine that works without drawing on an external energy source, something you can tap for power without having to keep feeding power to it. We could use superconductors for power transmission without loss, for giant computers, for more efficient motors and generators—except for one small problem."

"Which is?"

"The fantastically low temperatures that have to be maintained in order to have superconductivity in the first place. In theory, some elements should be superconductive at room temperature, but nobody has managed to translate that theory into practice yet, even after forty years of research. So it's necessary to rig huge refrigerating devices to provide temperatures twenty degrees or less above absolute zero, which is colossally expensive. To run a superconductive motor on Earth we have to put more energy into the system, by way of refrigeration, than we could hope to get out of it, and that's hardly practical. But on Pluto there's no refrigeration problem. The natural temperature there is one at which superconductivity exists. All right. Into our cubic crystal structure of silicon and cobalt we introduce, somehow, an electrical current. The spark of life! Instead of the biochemical energy generated by Earth-type life-forms, it's electrical energy—but it's still energy. Which persists indefinitely, thanks to superconductivity. Our Plutonians may look like lumps of metal, but they're alive and probably close to immortal. I can picture them paddling around slowly in the methane seas, pausing for a gulp whenever their metabolism demands some refreshment. They might have liquid helium in their veins, giving them the special advantages of superfluidity—"

"Superfluidity?" Fancourt said.

"Below 2.18 degrees absolute and under high pressure, helium becomes a very strange fluid that can pass through openings of incredibly small size, that can creep up the side of a glass vessel in defiance of gravity, and do a number of other extremely odd things. Helium at that temperature is known as Helium II; 'blood' made of Helium II might be an ideal carrier of nutrients through the body of a non-organic creature unable to pump a conventional fluid from one part of itself to another."

Fancourt looked doubtful. But he went past the point without challenging it and said, "What about reproduction? Can your silicon-cobalt methane-drinking Helium-II-blooded beasts reproduce themselves?"

"Why not?" Bill said. "I imagine that reproduction would be an uncommon event on Pluto. Since practically nothing can kill the Plutonians, they'd better not have much of a reproductive rate, or there'd be so many of them that they'd cover the entire planet ten deep. But I picture their reproduction as a kind of budding. The parent Plutonian constantly absorbs silicon and cobalt from the sea, which contains many suspended elements just as Earth's seas do; and when the parent reaches a certain size, a metallic 'whisker' might sprout on its surface. Over a few thousand years the whisker would fill out, gaining in size by absorbing molecules of cobalt silicate from the parent. When it attains certain minimum mass, it breaks free and takes up independent life, drifting through the ocean and foraging for its own food. The electrical spark of life is transferred automatically from parent to offspring, and sustains itself through superconductivity."

"How intelligent would you say these Plutonians could be?"

"I'm not prepared to guess at that," Bill said. "They might have minds of supercomputers, or they might be incapable of thought at all—nothing more than metabolizing and reproducing lumps of cobalt and silicon."

"Very interesting," Fancourt said. "Well, Bill Hastings, you've certainly concocted an impressive theory of how life could exist on a formidable planet like Pluto, and I hope you get the chance to find out some day how accurate your guesses were."

"It isn't very likely that I will. Not when it takes a century or so to make the round trip to Pluto. But—"

Fancourt cut him off. "Thank you, Bill. My guest tonight has been Denver's William Hastings, winner of the national essay contest on Life on Other Worlds, who has explained some of his ideas about the inhabitants of Pluto." He looked at the man in the control room. "All right, cut it here. We'll dub in the rest of it later." Getting to his feet, Fancourt said, "That's it, Bill. You gave me just what I wanted."

"But it was all old stuff, Mr. Fancourt! I mean, I covered it all in the interviews last summer, and—"

"That doesn't matter. You gave me just what I was looking for. I thank you kindly. And I imagine I'll be talking to you again soon. See you around, Bill."

Bill found himself smoothly but firmly being ushered out of the studio. He stood in the midst of the bustling Press Pavilion, trying to sort out his thoughts. While Fancourt had been interviewing him, he had felt confident, self-assured, in control of the situation; it had been the easiest thing in the world to meet the video man's deliberately dimwitted questions with explanations of how living things, of a sort, could endure the Plutonian environment. He knew that his theory was wildly speculative, but yet it all fit together solidly enough—the superconductive body crystals of silicon and cobalt, the electrical energy coursing eternally through resistance-free bodies, the "veins" in which Helium II flowed, the methane metabolism, the reproduction by whisker-budding.

Now, though, the interview was over. He didn't know why Fancourt had taken the trouble to interview him, nor why the Fair was suddenly aswarm with reporters; and he had his customary feeling that everyone around him knew more of what was going on than he did. It's not that I'm a dope, he told himself, or that I'm not alert. It's just that no one ever *tells* me anything.

He caught sight of Emily and called out to her as she sped by. "Hold it! I want to talk to you!"

"I can't talk now, Bill."

"Just for a minute."

"I've got to take these to the computer program center!" she said, indicating a stack of tape reels. "And you'd better get back to the Mars Pavilion double quick. Doc Martinson's been paging you for the past fifteen minutes."

"Did someone tell him I was here being interviewed?"

"I don't know," Emily said. "But he wants you in a hurry, that's sure!"

"Why are all these reporters here, Emily? At least tell me that much."

"I guess a big story's going to break."

"You guess? You guess? Come on, Emily, you *know*. You have to know. And—"

Too late. He was talking to himself. He watched her trim form retreating rapidly. Shaking his head in annoyance, he made his way out of the Press Pavilion through a throng of noisy, jostling reporters. As he emerged he caught the attention of a man wearing a Global News Service button on his lapel and said, "Can you tell me what all the fuss is about? Why is everyone here?"

"For the Regan press conference," the GNS man said.

"What conference?"

"Claude Regan called a press conference for two o'clock this afternoon in the Hall of the Worlds."

"And what's he going to announce?" Bill asked.

"How do 1 know? Nothing's leaked except that it'll be big news."

"It doesn't have to do with the closing of the Fair, does it?"

"Maybe yes, maybe no. It's not my business to guess the news, friend, just to report it when it happens."

The man disappeared into the confusion within. Bill headed for the uplevel ramp. That must be it, he thought.

Regan wouldn't pull 300 newsmen up from Earth to tell them something trivial. And the fact that he had chosen to make his mysterious announcement here at the Fair meant that the news must have to do with the Fair.

There was only one possible kind of news that the Fair was likely to be making these days, Bill knew: bad news. Here it comes, then. Regan is going to bring down the guillotine. Bill could hear it now: "In view of the extraordinarily high operating costs of the Columbian Exposition, and the unexpectedly poor public response, I regret to say that it will be necessary for us to close the Fair somewhat ahead of schedule. We are advancing the final day of activity here to April 12, 1993, which will round off six months of the most unusual and ingenious exposition in human history, and—"

—and everyone would go home. The End. Finis. Back to Earth for Bill Hastings, back to Mars for Moe and Joe and their families. It would be like having to awaken after a long and wonderful dream.

Bill reached the staff entrance of the Mars Pavilion and signalled for admission. The panel swung open; he slipped within and entered the laboratory, where he found Doc Martinson pacing like a caged beast. The little xenobiologist looked wild with fury.

"There you are!" he barked, turning on Bill. "Where have you been? Where in the name of the nine worlds have you been?"

"At the Press Pavilion," Bill said mildly. "I've only been gone half an hour."

"Doing what?"

"Roger Fancourt wanted to tape an interview with me."

Dr. Martinson's brow furrowed. "Roger who?"

Lou Pomerantz looked up. "Fancourt," he said. "News commentator."

"Never heard of him," said Dr. Martinson. Suddenly his hand shot out and caught Bill by the throat of his shirt. "A newsman? You've been talking to a *newsman?* About what?"

"My Pluto theories," Bill gasped. "He wanted me to go over everything again, in simple terms."

"That's all? You just talked about theories?"

"We didn't mention a thing that wasn't in my essay."

"All right. All right. I guess you couldn't have let anything slip, unless you know more than I think you do. Obviously this Fancourt knows plenty already, though. Come with me, fast! We've wasted enough time!"

They went buzzing out of the pavilion. Dr. Martinson was moving as though under rocket power across the plaza that led to the Global Factors Pavilion, and Bill worked hard to keep up.

Instead of taking the slidewalk to the exhibit area once they were within the Global pavilion, they turned to the side and went up an inconspicuous staircase that led into a balcony Bill had never noticed before. Passing through two sets of swinging doors, they halted in front of a door guarded by a burly, expressionless man in the uniform of the Fair security forces. Dr. Martinson gave his name and presented his identity plate to a scanner; the guard stepped aside and the door swung open.

Bill looked into a luxuriously decorated room with glossy wood-paneled walls and shimmering, iridescent curtains; a long table of what appeared to be polished marble occupied most of the center of the room, and about it sat a dozen well-dressed men of middle years, bristling with their own importance. To Bill it seemed like a dream-fantasy of a corporation's executive chamber.

The man at the head of the table was Claude Regan.

"Hello, Bill," he said amiably. "Won't you sit down? And you too, Dr. Martinson. Have you said anything to him about our little project, Dr. Martinson?"

"Not a word."

"Fine," Regan said. "I like to spring surprises."

Bill lowered himself uncertainly into a miraculously comfortable chair that seemed to have been designed especially for him. All eyes in the room were on him. It began to seem more and more like a dream—the one in which the dozen most important men on Earth summon you to a meeting where they tell you, "You alone can save the planet, Bill Hastings!"

The room was very silent.

After an endless moment Claude Regan said, "Bill, how would you like to go along on an expedition to Pluto?"

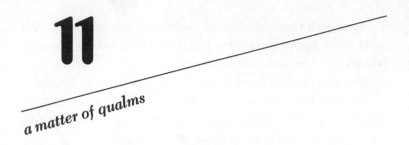

11

a matter of qualms

It was hard to see why Claude Regan would want to go to so much trouble to play a not very funny joke on one not very important employee of the Columbian Exposition. For Regan to assemble all these dignified-looking men in this imposing room, to have Doc Martinson hustle him breathlessly over here on such a pretense of urgency, to stand up amid tense silence as if about to reveal something of cosmic significance, and then to say something as foolish as what he had just said—it was beyond all comprehension. Even dreams make better sense than that, Bill thought.

Bill said quietly, "Sir, Pluto is more than three billion miles from here just now. It would take something above 45 years for an expedition to get there. I'd be about 120 years old when I came home. I don't think the odds on my living to 120 are very good."

Regan smiled. "You're right that it would take close to a century for the round trip, Bill. By conventional rocket transport, that is. Do you know how long the trip would take under continuous acceleration, though?"

"There's no way to keep a spaceship under continuous acceleration all the way to Pluto."

"Just suppose we could do it. How long would the trip take?"

Bill considered it. An ordinary spaceship fires its rockets until it gets up to the proper velocity for escape from Earth. Then it halts further acceleration and coasts along through space, courtesy of Newton's First Law, until the time comes to start up the engines again for deceleration and landing. The periods of acceleration at the beginning of the trip and deceleration at the end are extremely brief; most of the time of the voyage is spent in free fall. The chemistry of rocket fuel, Bill knew, dictated such an arrangement. A rocket would have to carry millions of times its own weight in fuel in order to keep the engines on all the way to Pluto; and no rocket ever built could get off the ground in the first place with such a load. The most efficient fuel yet developed could not be carried in sufficient quantities to permit more than a brief time of acceleration.

Under *continuous* acceleration throughout the whole spaceflight, though, a ship could attain fantastic speeds. A thrust that provided a steady acceleration of one gravity would build up velocity at a rate of 32 feet per second— which meant that the ship would be traveling about 22 miles per hour in its first second of flight, 44 miles per hour after two seconds, 66 miles per hour after three seconds, and so on. At that rate, the escape velocity of 25,000 miles per hour would be reached in less than 20 minutes, certainly a leisurely pace compared with that of a standard rocket taking off at a 5-G acceleration. But if the 1-G acceleration continued indefinitely, velocity would keep on increasing at that same modest rate of 32 feet per second until in short order the ship was traveling at millions of miles an hour.

At the end of the first day the velocity would be not quite two million miles an hour.

At the end of the first week the velocity would be more than thirteen million miles an hour.

On the tenth day of the voyage alone, the ship would travel almost half a billion miles—thus covering more than the entire distance from Earth to Jupiter in a single day.

"At 1-G all the way," Bill said, "I'd guess it would take about three weeks to reach Pluto."

"Close enough. The actual figure is eighteen days," said Regan.

"But of course it's impossible for a ship to carry enough fuel to let it keep accelerating for eighteen days."

"A conventional rocket couldn't do it." Regan agreed. "How about a nuclear-powered ship able to convert 80% of its fuel to thrust energy?"

"If we had such ships, sir, we could get them up to enormous velocities. But we don't."

"We do," said Regan softly.

He signalled with the tips of two fingers. The room darkened; a screen appeared in front of the magnificent draperies; an unseen projector hurled upon it a weird and somber landscape.

Instantly, intuitively, Bill realized that he was seeing Pluto.

It might just as easily have been Antarctica in mid-winter. What he saw was a broad plateau of ice sloping down to a grim ocean packed with jostling floes. The only light was an artificial one spearing out from the vicinity of the camera. No moon was in the black sky, just the hard dots of stars. The ice of frozen atmospheric gases, Bill knew, would look no different to him on film than the ice of frozen water; but yet there was something terribly alien about this desolate scene.

The camera began to pan along the lifeless beach. On and on it ran, following the line of the shore, turning occasionally to give an image of the dead sea, still, unstirred by winds. The motionlessness of that sea was eerie and frightening. This was a planet that received hardly any sunlight, and so had virtually no temperature differential from pole to pole: it was the same everywhere, just a few degrees above absolute zero. And so a deadly atmospheric stillness prevailed. Nowhere did warm air rush upward and cold air come sliding in to fill the gap. This was a planet that had never known a breeze; this was a sea that had never seen a wave.

Bill shivered with awe.

The camera traveled onward, and the desolation became more apparent. No, this could never have been a winter view of Antarctica; this could only be a world at the edge of the Solar System, on the rim of eternal night. How had they done it? What cleverness had created this ghastly movie? They had missed no detail; now and then the screen even showed the metal legs of the walking space-probe that presumably had taken these pictures.

On. On. Through a lifelessness beyond all understanding.

Then the camera halted and swiveled on its mounting, pointing once more to the sea, and out of the lifelessness came life. Gripping the arms of his chair in astonishment, Bill watched five things that might have been crabs come scuttling up out of that terrible sea.

There was no way of telling their true size, for nothing on the picture provided any sense of scale. The creatures could have been huge as boulders, tiny as pebbles. They were dome-shaped, squat, glossy; they looked solid and massive; they dragged themselves ashore on small half-hidden legs and rested there, forming a ragged circle. The camera's eye scanned them as though from a great height. Raging, Bill silently begged the machine to stoop, to give him a closer view; but it did not, and after only a few moments it moved on, continuing its mindless survey of the empty beach.

The lights came on.

Bill was trembling. He felt as though Pluto had reached out across billions of miles to tinge him with a fearful chill.

But—how? *How?*

Regan said, "You're the 50th person to see that film so far, Bill. It was taken last month by one of the mobile units of the unmanned first Pluto probe. We have about 11 hours of film altogether, but this is the only one that shows anything except ice and sea."

"First—Pluto—probe—" Bill muttered. "I don't understand. It's a joke, isn't it? You're trying out some new World's Fair exhibit on me. A mockup of a Plutonian landscape—"

"No mockup. It's the real thing," said Regan. "Global

Factors has been secretly working on a nuclear-powered spaceship for the past eight years, under government contract. We flight-tested the engine a year ago and achieved virtually complete conversion of fuel to energy. That allowed continuous acceleration for indefinite periods. Since then we've built several full-scale transport ships and quietly sent them out. Naturally, no agency monitoring the takeoff would have any way of calculating the real destination. One of the ships is on its way to Alpha Centauri at this minute—man's first star probe, Bill. By now it's reached its maximum velocity, 600 million miles an hour, 98% of the speed of light. But we won't have any news from it for a long while. It'll reach the Alpha Centauri system about four and a half years from now, and any messages it sends back won't get here for another four or five years. We've had quicker results from our Pluto probe. It made a perfect trip in a little under eighteen days, went into orbit around the planet, and dropped a dozen mobile surveyors that relayed pictures. More was learned about Pluto in one afternoon than in the whole six decades since its discovery. When the job was done, the probe came back. Now we're ready to send a second expedition—a *manned* expedition. Seven men. We're holding one of those seven slots open for you, Bill."

"No offense meant, Mr. Regan, but I can't believe any of this!"

"I can understand that. You aren't dreaming it, I assure you."

Bill shook his head. "It's too far out, though!"

"Pluto? Yes, of course."

"No. I mean this thing about my going. Look, sir, I'm not a scientist. I don't even go to college yet. If there's room for only seven men, shouldn't those seven be professional astronauts and scientists, the best-trained men in their fields?"

"Six of them will be," Regan said. "We have special reasons for wanting you to be the seventh. You saw those things crawling around at the edge of the sea?"

"Yes."

"They're Plutonians, obviously. Most scientists agreed that life wasn't possible at temperatures near absolute zero, but you worked out an ingenious explanation of how living creatures could exist in such conditions. The camera couldn't tell us whether the Plutonians really are constructed in anything like the way you suggested; *but we know that they're there*. The whole nation thinks of you as the boy who said there was life on Pluto. You're publicly identified with the subject. Think of the impact it'll make, Bill. Two hours from now I'm going to hold a press conference at the Hall of the Worlds to reveal the success of the Pluto probe and to announce that a manned expedition is about to depart. The expedition, I'll say, is going to stop at the World's Fair on its way out, in order to pick up the brilliant young man whose remarkable guess inspired the whole enterprise—yourself. You'll be the representative of American youth on the voyage: the first teenager to travel beyond the orbit of Mars! You've earned a slot on that ship, Bill. Everyone will agree with that. And everyone will thrill to your adventures on Pluto!"

A good many things were falling into place for Bill as he listened to Claude Regan's enthusiastic words. Now he understood why Regan had known the details of his essay, that time on Opening Day when they had met in the Mars Pavilion. He could remember what Regan had said that day: *"I'm sure Pluto has all sorts of surprises for us. If I have anything to say about it, we'll be exploring it sooner than most people expect. And perhaps you'll be going along, William."* Bill had discounted that speech as no more than polite chitchat; but Regan must have been ready to launch the secret unmanned Pluto probe just about then, and perhaps had even already selected Bill for the first manned expedition.

And then, just this morning, Roger Fancourt's puzzling insistence on interviewing him about his Pluto ideas. It hadn't made any sense; but clearly Fancourt had picked up some advance tip on Regan's Pluto expedition, and wanted a fresh tape of Bill in the can as background material for his show on the night the big story broke.

There was something unconvincing, though, about what Regan was saying. Maybe it was inspiring to send Bill Hastings, the All-American Boy, off to Pluto, but Bill still couldn't see it. Historic space expeditions simply weren't run that way. It was one thing to let the winner of a high school essay contest spend a year at a World's Fair in space, and another thing entirely to put him aboard the longest and most significant voyage in human history. There *had* to be a hidden angle.

As Regan went on talking, Bill began to see what it was.

The flamboyant little promoter was saying, "And while you're gone, Bill, we'll be engaged in a round-the-clock crash program to build a new pavilion here that exactly duplicates the conditions of gravity and temperature found on Pluto. So when you return with your cargo of live Plutonians, we'll be able to offer the world a second amazing attraction—not only the Old Martians, but also the incredible life-forms of the Solar System's most distant planet!"

Bill understood it all, now.

This was a gigantic publicity stunt to save a faltering World's Fair. No doubt the nuclear spaceship itself had been under development long before Claude Regan had ever imagined he was going to be involved with the Fair; but the rest was pure showmanship. Sending an unmanned probe to Pluto even before Uranus and Neptune had been explored might well have been inspired by his own essay, he realized: Regan, looking for a big new attraction for his Fair, was gambling that Bill's ideas were right and that little Pluto might hold life, whereas the nearer and bigger planets did not. And dispatching a manned expedition so soon, without going through the usual test period of several years using unmanned vehicles, could only have been dictated by the financial troubles of the Columbian Exposition. In theory this was a government project; but the billions of dollars controlled by Regan and Global Factors gave him the status of a government-within-the-government. The Mars Pavilion alone had not been enough to keep the Fair running, though it had stirred a temporary excitement at the beginning. A Pluto Pavilion beside it, however, would be an irresistible draw, and the Fair would come to life again. Bill's own presence on the expedition, he knew, was hard to defend scientifically, but it would make for marvelous publicity. BOY WONDER BLASTS OFF FOR PLUTO, stuff like that. The public couldn't work up much emotional identification with astronauts and professors, but it would follow every detail of Bill's adventures in high fascination.

They want to *use* me, Bill thought. And I don't like it.

Regan went on, "We estimate that you'll be gone a little over a month. The voyage should take fourteen or fifteen days each way, because the flight plans calls for an acceleration of one and a half G's instead of one. Not only will that save a little time, but it'll get the members of the expedition accustomed to the heavier gravitation on Pluto, where unusually high planetary density produces a grav of something like 1.7 Earthnorm, even though Pluto is smaller than Earth. Then we figure on three or four days' reconnaissance of Pluto—less, perhaps, if you can find the Plutonians faster. If you leave next week, as planned, you'll be back here early in April, just in time to give the second six months of the Fair a terrific sendoff."

The more Regan said, the less Bill liked the whole idea.

He looked around the room, letting his gaze move along the row of portly, prosperous-looking men. Who were they? They hadn't said a word; they simply sat here as part of the background scenery. The board of directors of Global Factors, maybe? High government officials? Space experts? They didn't look bright enough to be scientists. He looked at them, and they stared back at him; and finally he was looking at Claude Regan again.

Stripped of the fancy phrases about venturing into the unknown, the expedition presented itself to Bill as little more than a hunting and trapping operation. They were going to zoom to the outer edge of the Solar System and back merely so they could catch a few Plutonians to dress up Claude Regan's World's Fair.

Put on those terms it seemed hideous. Bill already knew of the moral qualms the xenobiologists had had about putting Old Martians on display at the Fair; now the same thing was going to be done to Plutonians, and, with great fanfare and buildup, they were asking him to co-operate in the second kidnapping..

Was it right? Should he get mixed up in anything so sordid?

A burst of anger rose in him, and he came close to shouting to Regan that he could find somebody else to go to Pluto. But he stopped himself in time.

For an endless moment conflicting thoughts streamed through his head.

Were the Plutonians intelligent beings, as the Old Martians were, with personalities, identities, character? Or were they primitive creatures no more intelligent than the crabs they resembled?

Would he consider it an outrageous act of kidnapping if a scientific expedition went to Alaska or Africa and collected some hitherto unknown type of crab for exhibition at the New York Aquarium?

Did it make any sense to refuse to go to Pluto on moral grounds, then, without knowing anything more about the Plutonians than that they existed? And did it matter that Claude Regan's motives for sponsoring the expedition were tainted with commercialism and hucksterism, so long as he would have a unique opportunity to take part in a fantastic adventure?

He didn't know. He was pulled in a dozen directions at once.

They were all staring at him. Bill ran his tongue over suddenly dry lips and said, "I'd like some time to think about all of this, sir."

Regan looked astounded. But he recovered quickly and said, "Naturally. We've sprung something pretty overwhelming on you. Why don't you go off by yourself for half an hour or so and get your thoughts sorted out?"

"I had two or three days in mind," Bill said.

With an almost imperceptible shake of his head Regan dismissed that possibility. "There isn't enough time for that," he said. "The press conference will be starting soon. Before that, we want you to talk to your parents. You'll need their permission, naturally, and so we've arranged a call to be put through to them in an hour. Don't think that we're stampeding you, but you understand that there's a time element involved."

"All right," Bill said, feeling uncomfortably like the victim of a stampede despite Regan's assurances. "Half an hour, then. Can I have a few minutes to talk to Dr. Martinson, too?"

"Of course." Regan gestured grandly; Doc Martinson rose from his seat and went into the hall with Bill.

The ferocity was gone from the scientist's expression. "You're all turned around inside, aren't you, Bill? I can imagine what it must be like."

"You could have given me some warning—"

"Impossible. I was under orders to get you to the meeting without hints."

"Doc, what should I do?"

"I know what I'd do if I were in your place. I'd go without thinking twice about it."

"But there are some ugly aspects. Like linking a voyage of exploration to a commercial exhibit at a World's Fair. And like kidnapping the inhabitants of another planet."

The scientist sighed. "I've heard all that stuff before, son. We fought it out last summer over bringing the Old Martians here."

"Yes, I know. I've discussed it with Lou Pomerantz and

some of the other staffers. And—"

"If you think that working for Claude Regan is dirty," Dr. Martinson said, "then you must think I'm covered with muck."

"I didn't say—"

"No, you didn't. Listen, Bill, I don't pretend that this is a simple matter, or that there are any easy answers. You're up against a good-sized moral problem, though it's not quite the same as the one we were facing. But my advice is to look at things in the least complicated way. Forget all the promotional hoopla that's going to surround the voyage. Forget that Regan is thinking mainly about bailing out his big show before it goes under. Just remember that you're being invited to go along on the greatest exploration in history. And that the Plutonians you're bringing back won't just be victims of a shameful abduction, but also invaluable scientific specimens, examples of the most extraordinary life-forms in the Solar System. If you had the deciding voice, would you try to prevent those specimens from becoming accessible to science?"

Put in those terms, Bill decided, it didn't seem so monstrous.

"Of course not," he said.

"Then why turn Regan down?"

Bill nodded. After a moment he said, "Will *you* be going?"

"Not this time. I've got enough to do running the Mars Pavilion."

"But there's got to be a real xenobiologist in the crew!"

"There will be," Dr. Martinson said. "Lou Pomerantz."

"He hates Claude Regan, though!"

"Will you stop complicating things? Lou isn't going

out there to make Regan happy. He's going there to explore Pluto. And the fact that Lou, whose conscience is so sore about the Mars Pavilion affair, is willing to go, ought to settle your own dilemma for you."

Cautiously Bill said, "Does Lou know anything about this expedition yet?"

Dr. Martinson laughed. "You're becoming a lot too suspicious, young man! Lou knows all about it. I brought him before Regan exactly an hour ago, while you were off with that newsman. He accepted the invitation on the spot."

"That's all I want to know," Bill said.

"Shall we go back inside and tell Regan you're all set?"

"Not just yet. I still want the rest of my half hour."

He left Dr. Martinson and made his way quickly toward the Press Pavilion. The chaos was worse than ever there—reporters swarming all over the place, signing in for the press conference—and Bill didn't try to fight his way in. From a communicator booth next door to the pavilion he phoned Emily and asked her to meet him outside it. She told him she was too busy; but he said it was urgent, and after some hesitation she gave in.

Moments later she appeared, walking briskly toward him.

"Well?"

"I've just come from the Global Factors Pavilion, Emily. From a meeting led by Claude Regan."

"He finally broke it to you, eh?"

"Broke what?"

"You know," she said.

"And so do you. Come on: what was it he asked me?"

She smiled. "To go on the Pluto expedition."

"Yes. The Pluto expedition. I suppose you've known about it for weeks!"

"Only since yesterday," Emily said. "Yesterday afternoon, when we did up the advance transcripts of his speech for the press conference."

"You could have told me," he said ruefully.

"Ten to one you wouldn't have believed me. Anyway, it would have been unethical and dishonest and pretty lousy, besides. I'm not supposed to take unfair advantage of my privileged position by divulging top-secret news."

"How did Roger Fancourt find out what was up, then?"

"Not through me," Emily shot back at him. She seemed to mean it, too.

"Okay. Skip it," he said. "What I really wanted to discuss with you is whether I should go at all."

She blinked in amazement. "Why in the name of Saturn's rings shouldn't you go?"

Words tumbled out of him. He sketched the situation in all its complexity, stressing his dislike of Claude Regan's cynicism and his unwillingness to get mixed up in the kidnapping of possibly intelligent creatures from their native world. When he finished, Emily stared at him in silence for a moment, and said at last, "Would you be happier if there weren't any Pluto expedition at all, and the Fair folded up from lack of business?"

"No."

"Do you think scientific research is evil?"

"You know I don't."

"Are you afraid to go?"

"Of course not!"

"That covers everything," Emily said.

"I guess it does," he agreed. "I better go back and tell

Regan I'm available."

"You're sure, now?"

"Positively. And thanks for helping me make up my mind."

"Your mind was made up from the beginning," she told him. "You were just playing games with yourself. But have a good trip, anyway. And look me up when you come back."

"You know I will," he said. "Well, so long, now."

"Just a minute," she said, and caught his wrist, and pulled him close to her. Their lips met, and there was nothing sisterly about her kiss this time. When they parted, he felt as if the Satellite's gravitation had suddenly been cut off and he had been plunged into free fall.

"That was for luck," she said softly, and turned, and went back toward the Press Pavilion without another word.

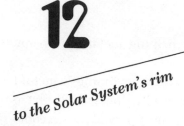

12

to the Solar System's rim

The call to his parents had already been set up by the time he returned to Regan at the Global Factors Pavilion, and they were waiting on the line. That was something of a surprise, since ordinarily it took two or three days to reserve a circuit on one of the telephone relay satellites. Obviously when Claude Regan wanted a circuit, he got a circuit, and nothing said about advance reservations.

It was even more surprising to discover that his parents didn't object at all to his running off to Pluto in some new-fangled kind of spaceship.

They looked a little baffled about it all, of course, particularly his mother. But they knew the whole story before he came on the line, and from the way they spoke it was evident that someone had done an expert persuading job on them, possibly even Regan himself. They appeared so stunned by their son's summons to fame that they were unable to interfere.

"Take good care of yourself," his mother kept saying. "Be careful not to get a chill."

"When will you be back?" his father wanted to know.

"At the beginning of April."

"You'll call us then?"

"Of course."

"Can't you call when you get to Pluto?" his mother asked.

"Maybe there's a way of relaying a message," Bill said. "But I won't be able to talk to you. It'll take five hours for anything I say to travel to Earth, and five hours for your words to get back to me, so we can't have much of a conversation."

He couldn't imagine how Regan had been able to win them over so thoroughly until his mother dropped a revealing remark near the end of the conversation. "We're so glad that you'll be getting away from the World's Fair for a while, sweetheart. I've never felt it was safe to be aboard that thing."

Bill smothered a laugh. She was still so worried about sabotage at the Fair that she preferred him to be on board a nice safe spaceship, heading toward Pluto at ten or fifteen million miles an hour!

His mother and his father told him over and over how proud of him they were, and he told them not to worry about him, and Claude Regan, who was standing by, began to look impatient. Finally Bill brought the conversation to an end. As he hung up Regan said, "We'll be running taped excerpts from it on every network tonight."

They hurried across to the Hall of the Worlds for the

press conference. The pavilion had been closed to the public most of the day, it turned out, so that everything could be prepared; and a few hundred disgruntled-looking fairgoers were gathered outside, as if hoping that they'd somehow get to see the celebrated exhibit after all. Reporters were being allowed in on presentation of admission passes, and as each one got past the security guards a round of booing rose from the onlookers. They began to boo again as Bill, accompanied by Regan and the rest of the group that had been at the meeting in the Global Factors Pavilion, approached. But the boos changed to excited whispers: "There's Claude Regan! Regan! Regan!"

Inside, rows of folding chairs had been set up on the floor of the Great Hall, spoiling the awesome effect of its cavernous vastness, and the place was packed with reporters. They occupied every available bit of space. As Regan led the way to the podium, some men began to file from an inner room at the back. It turned out, moments later, that they were the other members of the crew of the *Pluto I*.

Regan spoke briefly but with tremendous impact. First he had the motion pictures of Pluto shown on a vast screen near the front of the hall; Bill stared again at that bleak landscape, at those eerie crablike creatures crawling up the icebound beach.

"What you have just seen," Regan said quietly, "are the first films of the surface of Pluto."

He let the implications of that sink in. An immense gasp rose from the audience. You didn't need to be an expert on space to know that no one had expected Pluto to be reached in the twentieth century.

Regan went on to explain the background of the nuclear spacedrive and the theory of continuous acceleration. "It is possible," he said, "to make a round trip voyage to the limits of the Solar System in less than a month. We have transformed space travel. We have created a means of transportation that is even farther beyond today's conventional rockets than the modern interplanetary transport rockets are over the first rickety plane of the Wright Brothers. The Solar System lies open to us now, and the stars themselves no longer seem appallingly distant. To mark this epoch-making step in man's conquest of the universe, a manned exploratory expedition will be launched next week—not to Jupiter, not to Saturn, but to the last outpost of the Solar System, to the forbidding planet whose surface you have just glimpsed—to Pluto itself!"

Now Regan called forth the seven men who would make that historic journey. Three of them were astronauts who had been working in the test program for the nuclear ship—Commander Leonard Spencer, designated the captain of the *Pluto I*, Colonel Dave Abrams, and Lt. Colonel Martin Washington. One was a geophysicist, Dr. Theodore Santell of Harvard. One was an astronomer, Lee Burton of Luna Observatory. The sixth man was Lou Pomerantz, representing the science of xenobiology.

The seventh was Bill.

Regan made a point of saving Bill for last. The newsmen must have been expecting the last slot to go to some world-renowned personage, perhaps a famous novelist or philosopher; and when Regan produced the winner of the high school essay contest, the gasp of surprise was nearly as great as when the shots of Pluto had flashed on the screen. Only Roger Fancourt seemed unamazed. Bill saw him sitting in one of the front rows, grinning broadly.

Regan said, "It was Bill Hastings' stunning theory of the nature of life on Pluto that led us to attempt our unmanned reconnaissance of the ninth planet. That theory, as you've seen, has been magnificently confirmed by the pictures taken by our mobile surveyors. Therefore it seems only fitting to send Bill on the Pluto expedition as the representative of all the young people of the world, the bright, questing spirits who will in days to come be extending the dominion of mankind to the stars."

It sounded, Bill had to admit, downright impressive. He could almost believe it himself.

Regan explained next that one purpose of the expedition was to collect samples of Plutonian life. (He did not reveal that this would be the main purpose of the expedition.) He told how the Plutonians would be housed in a special new World's Fair pavilion that would be designed to duplicate the inhospitable environment to which they were accustomed. Just so no one would overlook the point, Regan made it several times: the Plutonians, he stressed, would be going on public exhibition at the Fair early in April, and in view of the expected rush to see them, it would be advisable to book reservations immediately.

That struck Bill as an awfully long gamble. Regan's announcement was certain to push Fair attendance down in March, since no one would want to come in the next few weeks when by waiting a little longer he could see the creatures from Pluto. And if the expedition failed and no Plutonians went on display at all, the effect on the Fair's finances was sure to be catastrophic. But, he reflected, it was Regan's profession to gamble on long shots, and his record so far indicated that he knew what he was doing.

When he was through with all he had to say, Regan

turned the conference over to the seven crewmen of the *Pluto I,* adding that because of time problems no interviews would be granted with individual members of the crew. Roger Fancourt's grin grew even broader. He would be the only one, then, with a recent tape of Bill to show tonight!

A question period started. About a third of the queries were directed at Commander Spencer, and dealt mainly with the way the nuclear spaceship operated and the speed at which it traveled. Another third of the questioning was aimed at Bill. The reporters wanted to know the details of his Pluto theory, mostly, but also something of how it felt to be the first teenager to explore the distant realms of the Solar System. "I don't know," Bill said simply. "I haven't explored anything farther from Earth than the World's Fair, yet. But I can say that I feel tremendously humble and grateful for my opportunity, and that I'll be going out there with my eyes wide open, trying to see everything that's there to see."

Regan beamed at him from the sidelines. Evidently he had said the right thing—a good quote for the evening news programs.

Bill fielded most of the other questions expertly enough. Once he got off into a long explanation of superconductivity as he thought it would apply to life on Pluto, and had to be rescued from what was becoming a monolog he could not end; but generally he gave brief, crisp answers. The question period lasted forty minutes and then was abruptly brought to a halt, even though dozens of reporters were clamoring for a chance to speak.

Bill and his fellow crewmen were hustled out a back way.

That afternoon he started to discover that from here until the day of departure he was not going to be allowed to have any private life at all. The first step was to move him out of the staff dorm and put him with the other six in a restricted sector of the Fair where no journalists or members of the public would be able to get to them. He was given half an hour to get his things packed. Nick Antonelli and Mel Salter helped; they both seemed astonished by the fame that had come to their bunkmate, and looked on him with awe. "I just want you to know," Nick said earnestly, "that I'm proud to have bunked with one of the first men to go to Pluto. That goes for Mel too. We're all proud of you. You ought to hear Emily talk!"

Bill wished he could hear Emily talk. But he had no chance to see her at all. That final good-bye kiss still tingled on his lips; he was looking forward already to an even warmer greeting from her on that triumphant day—seemingly millions of years in the future—when he returned safely from Pluto. He was starting to form some interesting plans for himself and Emily. He was still a little young for marriage, yes, but in three or four years he wouldn't be. And the fact that Emily came from one of the nation's oldest and most distinguished families wouldn't be all that much of a barrier, once he had put himself in the history books by voyaging to Pluto. Old and distinguished families had to start somewhere, didn't they? And some day people would brag that they were descended from the famous explorer William Hastings.

He told himself that he wouldn't feel quite so unable to cope with Emily's high-spirited, mischievous nature after the Pluto voyage. He had always been a little afraid of her, awed by her family's importance and by her own immense self-assurance; but he didn't plan to be quite so hesitant after Pluto. He could feel the changes in himself already, the growing awareness that he was someone of worth and talent, respected and sought-after by others.

The final briefings for the voyage, though, took up all his time in these last few days. Outsiders were firmly barred from the crew quarters, and he was unable even to make telephone calls. Regan had lowered a total-security curtain around the seven Pluto venturers. He was cut off, too, from the Mars Pavilion and its six alien inhabitants, visiting them for the last time on the busy afternoon after the press conference. Moe and Joe, May and Fay, Jack and Jill—he went among them once more in breathing-mask and thermal suit, and they put their small hands in his in complete trust, for by now they were old friends, and he tried to explain that he was going away. Moe, who was the only one with much of an English vocabulary, was able to grasp that. But he couldn't comprehend where Bill was actually going.

"To another planet," Bill said. "Very far away."

"To my world?"

"No, not yours, and not mine. A different world close to the stars."

It was too much for the Martian to follow. He knew of only two planets—his own and Earth. Venus, Jupiter, and Saturn were all visible to the naked eye from Mars, of course, but the Martians, spending their lives in underground caves, had no astronomical concepts at all, and the idea of "other worlds" was bizarre to them. Bill suspected that they thought of Earth itself as some strange and distant region of Mars; there was no way whatever that he could get through to them where Pluto might be.

But they understood that he was leaving them for a while, and the warmth of their farewells was unmistakable. "I'll miss you too," he said. "But I'll be back soon."

Now he plunged into a nearly round-the-clock indoctrination program for the Pluto mission.

Hardly any time was spent training him for service aboard the ship. He was shown the general layout and told where the controls were and where the power reactor was, but they gave him no operating instructions. As on any conventional spaceship, operations were largely automatic and computer-controlled; in case any manual operations were necessary, it would be the job of the three astronauts to handle them.

Bill's briefings concentrated on teaching him how to use a spacesuit and how to operate the land vehicles that the explorers would ride on Pluto's surface. The spacesuits were the standard insulated jobs worn by spacemen everywhere, but Bill had never worn one before, and he had to be trained to move efficiently while inside what amounted to a suit of flexible armor, and how to make use of the various communication and control devices the suit contained. He was somewhat shaken up to find that one of the most important elements of the spacesuit was its refrigeration unit. "Refrigeration on Pluto?" he yelped. Yes: the suit was so efficiently insulated against heat loss that the warmth generated by his own body would swiftly cook him if not dealt with.

The land vehicles were not quite standard items. In general structure they resembled the crawlers used for transportation on the Moon, on the surface of Mars, and in Antarctica—double-walled shells with a dead space of vacuum between the walls to cut heat radiation, and a silver coating on the inner surfaces to reflect heat back to the interior. But the temperature on Pluto was more than 100 °C. colder than anything encountered on the Moon even in the darkest part of the night there. Insulating against —270 °C. was not really much more of a technical challenge than insulating against —150 °C., but Pluto posed a special structural problem because of the tendency of many materials to change their physical properties entirely near absolute zero. Some metals perfectly suitable for Moon vehicles became hopelessly brittle; some plastics would turn to powder at the lightest touch. The crawlers had been redesigned using only materials capable of withstanding the lowest temperatures in the universe, and with such features as lubrication of external bearings by liquid helium.

At the end of the week a maintenance crew brought the *Pluto I* up from Earth. The nuclear ship was moored in a parking orbit a short distance from the Fair Satellite, since it had not been designed to make an airlock-to-airlock linkup with the Satellite after the fashion of the shuttle ships. Bill and his six crewmates were taken out by shuttle to inspect the spaceship. Spacesuit-clad, the seven men entered the shuttle ship. It broke its link with the Fair Satellite and headed out to match orbits with the *Pluto I*. The shuttle's blastoff from the Fair Satellite was more of a driftoff than a blastoff, since escape velocity from the Fair was practically zero. A man standing on the outer skin of the Fair Satellite could thrust himself into space with one good kick. So the shuttle freed itself with a gentle blast from its hydrogen jets; anything more than a moderate fizzing might have deranged the orbit of the Fair Satellite itself.

It took only a few minutes to maneuver into position near the nuclear ship. The vessel was a strange one, unusually long and narrow, with a ribbed surface that made it look like some kind of dinosaur. There was a bell-shaped passenger compartment at one end; at the other was the power section, with plenty of shielding in between to intercept stray alpha particles and other hard radiation. The familiar boosters of a conventional chemical-fuel rocket were missing altogether; in their place were the narrow vanes through which the nuclear engine would thrust the thin stream of radiation that moved it forward.

To enter the ship Bill made his first spacewalk. Lt. Col. Washington, one of the astronauts, led the way, stepping out of the airlock of the shuttle ship and using his backpack jets to send him toward the nuclear vessel. He carried a line from ship to ship and fastened it in place; then the others went across holding the line.

Bill felt a surge of wild panic as his turn to leave the shuttle approached. Was his spacesuit properly sealed? Would he lose his grip on the line and go drifting off into the abyss of darkness? Would dizziness overwhelm him and force him back into the shuttle quivering with fear?

All nervousness fled when the moment came. He reached forward, grasped the line with his gloved hand, and gave a gentle tug; the effort drew him forward and he found himself in the middle of the void, with nothing under his feet except the entire universe.

There was no "up" here and no "down." He seemed motionless, although he knew that he was hurtling through space at thousands of miles an hour, relative to any fixed point on the Earth. The huge globe of the Earth lay to his left; the coppery skin of the Fair Satellite lay between him and it; the Moon seemed within easy reach, with every crater on its pockmarked face sharply outlined; and stars were everywhere, glittering like diamonds strewn across the infinite black back-drop. He felt no uneasiness now. Halfway between one ship and the other he deliberately let go of the line. He hung suspended in the void, staring down at his booted feet and at the planet Earth, 50,000 miles beyond them. He had never felt so absolutely free before. There was no danger of his "falling" toward Earth, unsupported though he was; rather, he "fell" at a graceful pace toward the nearby nuclear ship, since the momentum he had acquired by tugging on the taut line was enough to keep him going in that direction. Easily, smoothly, he drifted toward the ship in a tight orbit. When he neared the open airlock he caught the line again and pulled himself into the ship.

For the next three days the training sessions were held aboard the *Pluto I*. Bill rapidly grew familiar with shipboard routine, and spent so much time in his spacesuit that it seemed like a perfectly natural garment to him. Quarters aboard the ship were going to be cramped, but not very much more so than in his dormitory bunk—and there wouldn't be soiled clothing strewn all over the place here, or musical instruments taking up every available bit of wall. The computer would thaw and cook their meals for them—prepackaged stuff that wasn't likely to be enormously less appetizing than the food served at the staff cafeteria at the Fair. He would manage to tolerate it. And two weeks later, he would be on Pluto.

Departure came with no fanfare whatsoever. One day at the beginning of March Commander Spencer announced that the training period was over and that they were going to leave. No reporters saw them off; the only thing resembling a ceremony was a telephone call from Earth in which President Hammond and Secretary-General Hannikainen wished them good luck. Claude Regan, who had also returned to Earth to attend to business matters, spoke briefly to each of them; then they suited up, took the shuttle out to the *Pluto I*, spacewalked across to the nuclear vessel, and settled in.

At noon Greenwich Standard Time on the 4th of March, 1993, the power reactor came alive in response to a computerized signal, and the *Pluto I* headed outward at an initial velocity of slightly less than thirty miles an hour. But the acceleration—the rate of change of speed—was constant at one and a half G's. Each second, the *Pluto I* was traveling about thirty-two miles an hour faster than it had been going the second before. Before the ship had been in motion two minutes, it was moving swiftly enough to get from New York to Los Angeles in an hour. By the fifteenth minute of the voyage the ship was moving at a pace that could have taken it completely around the world at the Equator in that same single hour. And by the end of the first day, the seven occupants of the *Pluto I* were streaking toward the depths of space many times faster than human beings had ever traveled before.

Bill felt no sensation of high speed. A spaceship is a self-contained world, and those inside it are no more aware of movement than people on Earth are of the turning of their planet on its axis. To Bill the *Pluto I* might almost have been standing still; the view through its ports showed only the stars, and even at a speed of millions of miles an hour the spaceship hardly seemed to be moving relative to the stars.

What he did feel was the gravity. The effect of G-and-a-half acceleration was to add 50% to his weight, without adding a thing to the muscles that he used to haul that weight around. It was suddenly an effort to take a step, to reach out a hand, even to sneeze. An ordinary space-flight began with really brutal gravitation—five G's or so, making you weigh half a ton and slamming you hard against your acceleration cradle—but quickly cut to utter weightlessness. Here there was neither the rough acceleration of a fast takeoff nor the weird release of free fall and null-grav; there was just the steady pull of a gravity half again as strong as normal, hour after hour, day after day.

The first few days were pretty bad; Bill and everyone else got musclebound and shortwinded. After that, one at least learned how to adapt to the extra pull, how to conserve energy and avoid any sudden muscle-straining motions. But it was never comfortable to live under the surplus half G; Bill felt as though he were buried in molasses up to his hips.

There wasn't much hard work to do. The ship virtually ran itself. On a conventional flight, where it was important to conserve fuel, everything had to be checked and rechecked before a ship was injected into its flight orbit. But the *Pluto I*, with an almost limitless fuel supply, could be corrected in midcourse if necessary without worry, and so all that needed to be done was to point it in the approximate direction of the place Pluto would be two weeks from departure time, and patch up any errors en route. Even at millions of miles an hour, there'd be ample time to get the ship back on course.

So the astrogator, Col. Abrams, simply looked over the

computer's info sheets every six or eight hours, and otherwise took no active part in directing the ship. Lt. Col. Washington, whose special province was the power system, looked in now and then on the monitors that controlled the reactor. Most of the others on board spent their time reading, sleeping, peering out the ports, or exercising in a stubborn attempt to build up their muscles in the heavy grav.

The astronomical show was spectacular only once, when glorious Saturn came in view. It would have been pleasant, Bill thought, to find the whole Solar System neatly lined up, so as they passed each planetary orbit in turn they'd have close-up views of Mars, Jupiter, Saturn, Uranus, and Neptune. But when they crossed the orbit of Mars the red planet was in opposition to them on the far side of the Sun. Jupiter, with his proud cluster of moons, was also so far down-orbit from them that they saw nothing. Saturn, at least, didn't fail them. They flashed by it going some thirteen million miles an hour, which wasn't exactly the pace for a leisurely inspection, but since their ship's orbit brought them within a million miles of Saturn at the closest point they were able to spend a couple of hours watching the ringed world grow nearer. Soon it was bigger than the Moon as seen from Earth: a gorgeous globe that swelled and swelled and swelled until it appeared to fill every porthole. They did the Saturn fly-by at an angle of 28° to the big planet's equator, which gave them a magnificent view of the three bands of rings whirling about Saturn's middle. Pale stripes of orange, yellow, pink, and red gases made Saturn seem like a huge globe of sucking-candy in space.

Their time of nearness to Saturn lasted only minutes.

One minute they were two million miles away, five minutes later they were at maximum approach, and in five minutes more Saturn lay a million miles behind. Even so, the enormous size of the sixth planet allowed them to have a splendid view for another half hour; then Saturn dwindled, became a colorful dot against the blackness, and was gone.

The next day they passed a major milestone in their flight: they were now one billion miles from Earth. It was time to start thinking about slowing the ship down, even though they were little more than a quarter of the way to Pluto.

Under constant acceleration of one and a half gravities, they would keep on gaining velocity at a rate of thirty-two miles an hour for each second that they kept the spacedrive turned on. They weren't very far into the fifth day of their flight, and already they were covering every four hours a distance greater than that from Earth to Mars. Another couple of days at this acceleration and they'd be doing 20,000,000 miles an hour, or close to half a billion miles a day.

At that rate they could reach Pluto in little more than a week. But when they got there they'd be going at a respectable fraction of the speed of light. It isn't easy to land a spaceship at a speed of better than 25,000,000 miles an hour. If they hit Pluto at anything like that velocity, they'd be carrying enough energy to blow the planet apart. $E = mc^2$ holds just as true for spaceships in flight as it does for atomic bombs; mass increases with speed, and mass, Einstein showed, can be a form of energy, and the energy packed into the *Pluto I* at these speeds was something to have nightmares about. They had to give up all that energy before they got to Pluto; they had to shed every speck of velocity by the time they landed on the ninth world's frigid surface.

So, as they neared the midpoint of their journey, the turnover point, the *Pluto I* went into a programmed flip-flop, somersaulting from acceleration to deceleration.

From the point of view of the ship's occupants, nothing had changed. The spacedrive still functioned like a miniature sun, converting matter to energy and squirting it out the vanes. The gravitational pull aboard ship remained one and a half G's. There was no period of free fall; a nuclear spacedrive had energy to waste, so why bother coasting? The difference was that the vanes of the *Pluto I* now were aimed sunward instead of Plutoward. The ship had turned around; it was using all its furious force as a brake instead of a forward thrust.

The ship began to slow down.

Deceleration proceeded at precisely the same pace as acceleration. The vessel lost velocity at the rate of forty-eight feet per second, which meant an almost negligible drop that became significant only as the seconds mounted into hours and the hours stretched into days. To reach turnover point they had zoomed up one side of a pyramid of velocity; now they were over the top and sliding down the other side, doing everything in reverse.

Slower . . . slower. . . .

Down to 20,000,000 miles an hour—still enough to cover twice the distance from the Sun to Mars between midnight and dawn. Down another 5,000,000 mph . . . another . . . down 2,000,000 mph more. . . .

They were three billion and some miles from home, out beyond the orbit of Uranus and practically at the frontier of interstellar space. Pluto was the destination, that shrunken ball of ice gliding dreamily through the great dark, and they slipped Plutowards at an ever-diminishing velocity, sliding into the humble speeds of a conventional rocketship, getting down now to the point where they could reckon their velocity in thousands instead of millions of miles an hour, ridding themselves even of those thousands as they neared Point Zero.

"There's Pluto," Lou Pomerantz said.

"God!" gasped the astronomer, Burton. "Who'd believe it? Pluto right in front of us!"

They peered through the ports. Outside, hanging near them in space, was the curving bulk of a small shining world, dimly reflecting the light of the distant sun from its frozen flanks. They could see continents—colossal plateaus of ice—broken by darker shapes, the vast expanses of methane seas. To Bill it was somehow far less amazing to be landing on Pluto than he had imagined, for it was so much beyond his own belief that he was here that he could scarcely absorb the reality of it. Yet here they were, at the Solar System's rim, farther from home than human beings had ever been before, cut off from the brightness and gaiety of Earth by billions of miles of nothingness.

Down they went. Down.

And made a perfect landing on the world at the brink of nowhere.

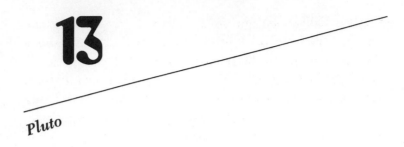

13

Pluto

They had come down near the eastern shore of the northern continent of Pluto's western hemisphere—in northern New Jersey, not far from New York City, if Pluto had been Earth. It was just where they wanted to be, for it was along this shore that the mobile surveyor had sighted the Plutonians.

The unmanned Pluto probe had brought back a photographic map of the planet taken by a quartet of spy satellites placed in orbit around it. It showed four continents of roughly equal size, two on each hemisphere, divided by two strips of ocean that girdled the planet around the equator and from pole to pole. That was an unimaginative geographical arrangement, Bill decided. Those four squarish blotches of ice-covered land lacked the irregular beauty of Earth's continents.

Why Pluto had continents and seas at all was one of the things the scientists wanted to discover. Dr. Santell, the geophysicist, had talked about it on the way out. The surface of Earth had been shaped by the fiery forces deep within the planet, which in mighty convulsions pushed mountains up and pulled continents apart. But did Pluto have the same kind of volcanic core? Earth's own moon had turned out to have a molten interior, cold and lifeless though it had seemed to those who viewed it from Earth. Were there surging rivers of lava within this icebound planet? Dr. Santell would not have much time to find out. There would be an opportunity only for preliminary checking during the hurried few days the First Pluto Expedition would spend here. They were under orders to collect specimens of Plutonian life and head back toward home as fast as possible; if any other scientific work got done, it would be strictly on a catch-as-catch-can basis. Lou Pomerantz had grumbled, "It's as though Columbus sailed across the Atlantic, stayed in the New World just long enough to grab the first three Indians he met, and rushed back to Spain." But orders were orders.

At a little past midnight, local time, the *Pluto I* came to rest on Pluto's surface. But "midnight" here was considerably different from midnight on Earth, since Pluto's dawn lay some three Earthside days in the future. It took almost a week, Earth time, for Pluto to make a single rotation on its axis. What passed for sunlight here would not become visible until they were nearly through with their work.

But it was summer at least. The sensors reported that the ground temperature at the time of landing was four degrees above absolute zero. The atmospheric temperature was a little milder—enough to keep the hydrogen-helium atmosphere from liquefying.

A lovely, balmy, tranquil summer evening on Pluto!

Under Commander Spencer's orders they swung into landing routine. First came a cautious checkout of the three land vehicles they had brought with them. A hatch opened high on the belly of the *Pluto I,* and the crawlers were carefully lowered to the ground by spring-mounted automatic cranes. Col. Abrams put the vehicles through their paces under remote control, running them gradually up to their maximum speed of forty miles an hour while getting telemetered reports on their performance. The insulation of the crawlers checked out nicely: internal temperature remained at the programmed level of 18°C., or almost 240° warmer than it was just outside the double shell. Mechanically the crawlers functioned well too. Abrams brought them back to the ship and they were hauled up again.

Now the spacesuits were checked out even more carefully. If a crawler's insulation failed, the men within still had their spacesuits to protect them; but the spacesuit was the last line of defense. The checkout took more than an hour. When it was over, they drew lots for the honor of being first on Pluto, giving their names to the computer to make a random pick.

It all seemed faintly silly to Bill. For him it was impressive enough to be on Pluto at all; to have been part of the first exploring expedition was a sufficient place in history; there was something childish about fretting over which of them would actually be the first one to plant his boots on Pluto's ice. The others seemed to feel the same way. Everybody was so elaborately unconcerned about who got the honor that each man would gladly step aside in anyone else's favor; but that way they could be doing an After You, Alphonse routine forever, and the random pick simplified the problem.

The computer decreed that Commander Spencer was to be the first Earthman on Pluto.

Lt. Col. Washington laughed. "That's going to look phony, all right! Everyone's going to think that he pulled rank on us because he's the commanding officer!"

Spencer shrugged. "Suppose you go first, then, Marty."

"Me?" Washington gasped in mock astonishment. "You want to bring us bad luck? The computer picked you."

"We can sign an affidavit that it was a legitimate random pick," said Dave Abrams. He nudged Spencer in the ribs. "Come on, Len, suit up and get yourself down there and plant the flag!"

Commander Spencer began to don his spacesuit.

He swung himself up into the exit hatch and extended the ladder.

They followed him down—Abrams, Burton, Hastings, Pomerantz, Santell, Washington. The world outside the ship was a field of white stretching to the horizon.

By the light of the ship's beam they raised the United Nations flag to symbolize the international status of all the worlds of space; no country could "claim" a planet the way whole continents had been claimed in the bad old days on Earth. Next the flag of the United States was raised, since the expedition was under American sponsorship. Bill scuffed nervously at the ice with the toe of one boot, trying to persuade himself that he was really on Pluto, and not at the South Pole. He looked toward the far-off sea, wondering what alien beasts it might contain.

They saluted the two flags; and finally Spencer produced a third one, a small flag bearing the corporate insignia of Global Factors. He made a wry face, indicating his distaste for this part of the ceremony, and spread the flag out on the ground. Claude Regan had to work in his commercial, Bill thought. Well, Global had built the ship and had put up some of the funds for the expedition, but even so this seemed to be going a little too far.

The flags looked awful, dangling limply from their posts. The Plutonian atmosphere was utterly still, and always would be. No one was ever going to see Old Glory rippling in the breeze on this planet.

When the little ritual was over, they got down to work.

Two two-man teams were going to take the crawlers out to search for Plutonian life: Bill and Dave Abrams in one, Pomerantz and Martin Washington in the other. Dr. Santell and Lee Burton, the astronomer, would remain near the ship, performing scientific experiments. Commander Spencer planned to stay aboard the *Pluto I*, manning the communications equipment and keeping everyone under remote surveillance.

They all returned to the ship to get the crawlers ready. Team A—Pomerantz and Washington—went through the checkout procedures first, with Bill and Dave Abrams helping. Once A Crawler had been sent through the hatch and lowered on the ground, Team B—Bill and Abrams— got to work. Bill entered B Crawler first, settling down at the rear. The cabin of the crawler was dome-shaped, with a 360° panel of vision screens; the entire dome was set upon a square platform that housed the drive mechanism and the crawler tracks. Abrams followed him in, taking the driver's seat; the cabin hatch was closed and dogged into place, triple-scaled for effective insulation.

Over the communication phones came Commander Spencer's voice, asking if they were ready.

"We're ready," Abrams replied.

"All right, B Crawler. Out you go."

The crane grips seized the vehicle and nudged it toward the rim of the hatch. Behind, the airlock door closed. B Crawler swayed a little as the crane lowered it to ground level. A Crawler was already well along on its way, heading southeastward toward the sea. The plan called for each of the crawlers to travel diagonally away from the landing area until it reached the sea; then A Crawler would turn north and B Crawler south, and both would proceed along the shore until they made rendezvous.

Abrams said into the audio mike, "We're up to maximum velocity and on our way, Skipper."

"Check," Commander Spencer replied. "I've got you on my tracking screens and I read you beautifully. Call in every hour, so I know you're still there."

Bill glanced at Abrams. "Why does he wants us to do that? He's got us telemetered automatically, right?"

"Sure. But he wants to hear our voices, too. He wants to make sure we're staying alert, and telemetry won't tell him that nearly as well as an hour-by-hour call-in."

Bill quickly understood why Spencer might be worried about their ability to keep alert. The journey was incredibly monotonous. There was no variation in the scenery: an endless iccfield spread out on all sides, unbroken even by hills. No boulders, no ponds, no trees, no landmarks of any sort broke the trackless wasteland. The crawler's headlights, eight of them set in an equidistant spacing around the middle of the vehicle, speared into the darkness, creating pools of light on the glassy surface of the ice. The glare was almost blinding, and produced a hypnotic effect; it was like traveling over a landscape of glittering mirrors. Even the motion of the crawler over the ice contributed to the dreaminess: the liquid suspension of the cabin on its tracks damped all movements down to a faint jounce, so that Bill was lulled by the sleepy rhythms as they rolled onward.

Abrams kept watch over his control panel, which relayed to him a steady sonar report on the area just ahead. Sonic beams, bouncing off the ice, warned him of any hidden flaws or crevasses. Bill, meanwhile, surveyed the surrounding region, peering intently in every direction as though expecting a war-party of Plutonians to come thundering down at them. He saw nothing—nothing but the crawler's own lights gleaming on the ice.

At a steady speed of forty miles an hour they rolled toward the sea. The ship had landed less than two hundred miles from the coast, and yet it was seeming to take forever to get there. Bill's patience was frayed by the time of the first hourly call-in. He had never imagined that forty miles an hour could be so eternally slow. It was an inchworm's pace. Just yesterday, slicing through space at a fantastic speed, they had spanned thousands of miles in the blinking of an eye, and now it was an endless business merely to cover a short distance like this. But everything was different now. They were planetbound, pinned down by gravity, limited by the requirements of a massive vehicle moving under difficult circumstances over slick ice. They crawled on. And on. And on.

This is Pluto, Bill told himself. I'm part of the grandest

adventure man has ever undertaken. How can I possibly be so bored?

He yawned. He struggled to keep his eyes open. That glare outside—the shimmer of light on the glassy ice—the wall of darkness beyond the reach of their beams—the throb of the engine, the soft purr of the air-recycling equipment, the sway of the cabin suspension—the emptiness, the unchangingness—everything conspired to cast a spell of dreams over him.

Dave Abrams was feeling it too. "We've got to keep talking to each other," he said. "It's too easy to lose concentration. Too easy just to go to sleep."

"Why is it happening so fast? An hour or two of monotony shouldn't do it."

"We've had two weeks of monotony. Sitting in a tin can going five million mph isn't all that different from sitting in another kind of tin can going forty mph. Our minds are overloaded with emptiness. And now—that constant glare out there—"

"Maybe we should cut the light," Bill suggested.

"And drive in the dark? I don't like that."

"But we've got the sonar to watch the road for us. And we don't have to worry about hitting telephone poles."

Abrams shrugged. "Okay, we'll try it."

He switched off the lights. Instantly the darkness came flooding in around them, reconquering the circular zone of brightness with which they had surrounded themselves. It hurt. The absence of the glare was as painful as the glare itself had been. Bill shut his eyes, kept them shut for a long moment, gradually opened them to the blackness. It was as if they had driven the crawler into a closet.

"I expected the stars to be brighter on Pluto," he said.

"So did I. It's this skimpy little atmosphere that cuts them out."

Bill nodded. Pluto lay wrapped in just a few wisps of hydrogen and helium—but the molecules of the gases making up the planet's atmosphere were packed close together, because of the intense cold. It made for a dense atmosphere—what there was of it.

They drove on in darkness for a while. Now both of them watched the control panel. The sonar had already shown them that Pluto's surface was deceptively pocketed with crevasses; the layer of frozen gases covering the ground was always near its melting point, so that as the planetary temperature rose and fell with changes in the orbital distance from the Sun, underground movements took place, vast blocks of ice slid against other blocks, and concealed instabilities were created. Bill knew that having the lights off made no difference in their ability to avoid tumbling into one of those crevasses. Only the sonar, pinging against the ice ahead of them, could spy danger. But the lights had given at least an illusion of safety.

The time for the second hourly call-in arrived. Abrams switched to external communications and told Spencer that all was well; then he stopped the crawler, looked at Bill, and said, "How'd you like to drive this bus for a while?"

"Sure thing."

They changed places. Bill ran his hands over the controls, getting the feel of them, and got the crawler moving. Driving it wasn't very different from driving an automobile: you keyed in the accelerator, kept your hand on the steering rod and your right foot on the brake, and sat back. The main difference was that Bill didn't need to worry much about holding his car on the road; there was no road, and he simply had to stick to an approximate northeastward course. Whenever he veered from course a light on the control panel would tell him, and so there wasn't even much challenge in steering.

After five minutes, though, he decided that he simply couldn't drive in the dark. "I'm switching the lights back on," he told Abrams, and nudged the button. Instantly the world about them blazed with the fierce reflected glare.

To fight back the terrible boredom they recited autobiographies. Bill went first, and found to his surprise that he had said all he could say after just a few minutes. Birth, upbringing, family background, hobbies, accomplishments, schooling, ambitions, the essay contest, the work at the Mars Pavilion, the astonishment of being picked to go to Pluto—that was William Hastings in a capsule. Abrams was nearly as concise, though he had lived nearly twice as long. He was 34, born in Indiana, raised in Ohio, with a B.S. in astronautics from Ohio State. He had gone into the Space Force straight from college, had served on the Moon and had made two voyages to Mars, was married, had two children, lived in Louisiana now, was delighted to be part of the Pluto team, and was looking forward to another six active years before Space Force regulations forced him into mandatory groundside work. It took him about ten minutes to sketch in the outlines of his life and career, and when he was finished they both lapsed into silence again.

When the third call-in came, they were a hundred miles out from the ship. Bill longed to get out and stretch his legs; sitting in this cramped cabin wasn't improving his patience any. But there was no way of leaving the crawler without emptying the vehicle of its atmosphere. Crawlers didn't come equipped with airlocks; if they unsealed the hatch, the air would flee in one quick whoosh, and for the rest of the journey they'd be riding around in an environment of Plutonian chill. There was nothing really dangerous about that as long as their spacesuits were functioning properly; but it was risky to have to depend on the spacesuits alone. Leaving the crawler was something to be done only as a last resort, this far from the ship.

So they sat tight. Midway through the fourth hour of the drive they stopped for a snack, which helped to kill the boredom. They opened radio contact with A Crawler and swapped gossip with Pomerantz and Washington, who were having the same troubles with the monotony of the long trek.

When B Crawler was six hours out from the base, word came from Marty Washington in the other crawler: "We've reached the sea."

"Do you see any Plutonians?" Bill asked.

"Sure," came the calm reply. "They're all over the beach, sunning themselves like lizards."

"Sunning themselves?"

"That's right. Crawling around by the millions. We got so many of them I can't see through the screens. Hey, Lou, what say we go out and catch ourselves a tubful? Have us a Pluto Fry for dinner!" Washington laughed. "And maybe save two or three for old Bill to see."

"Stop fooling around," Bill said. "Are there really Plutonians there?"

"You bet," Washington said. "Green ones, blue ones, pink ones. We got some with wings and some with long tails, and a few with orange horns, and—"

"If you won't give me a straight answer, put Pomerantz on. Lou? Lou, what's there? What do you see?"

"Not much," said Pomerantz. "Some nasty-looking ocean, is all."

"Plutonians?"

"So far only in the lively imagination of Lt. Col. Washington," Pomerantz reported. "But we'll give the neighborhood a good going-over as we move up the coast."

They broke contact. Bill wished he could step on the gas and force the crawler to speed seaward. But it was moving at its top speed. There was nothing he could do but sit and fidget until they came to the shore.

Half an hour later the ground began to slope away from them, and the sonar told them of a sharp drop in surface level just ahead. In a few minutes more the range of the headlights caught up with the range of the sonar, and they had their first glimpse of the Plutonian ocean.

It was disappointing. Bill remembered Regan's films of a gray, forbidding sea; but the camera had been able to see farther in the darkness than he could, and he was able to make out only the first few hundred feet of the "water," a dark, ice-flecked strip bordering the shining icy beach. That was no water out there, he realized, but a sea of liquid methane. Yet living creatures, he knew, moved in that deadly sea.

Halting the crawler a dozen yards from the edge of the sea, Bill turned to Dave Abrams, who was studying the vision screens, and said, "Do you see anything moving?"

"Zero."

"Me neither," Bill said. Slowly he swung the crawler around to line it up facing south, parallel with the shoreline. He looked at screen after screen until he had made a complete circle, and still nothing moved on the beach.

He said, "I guess we shouldn't expect to find Plutonians the minute we get here."

"If they're sea-dwelling creatures that only come up on land now and then," Abrams said, "we may have to hunt a long time for them. It may have been only the wildest bit of luck that the mobile surveyor saw them. We may not find them at all."

"Don't say that!"

"I'm just being realistic. We don't have much flexibility. We're working in the most hostile environment within four billion miles, and about all we can do is drive slowly down the beach and hope. There isn't a whole lot we can do to catch us some Plutonians unless they pop up right under our noses."

"If we don't find any along the shore," Bill said as he put the crawler into motion again, "we can try operating submerged for a while, can't we?"

Abrams looked gloomy. "We can try it, yes. With all the risks that that involves. If the sea floor turns out not to be solid, we can vanish awfully fast."

"We haven't vanished yet," Bill pointed out, "and we've crossed a couple of hundred miles of pretty tricky ice." He stared uneasily at the barren beach. They were gliding along at a couple of miles an hour, but nothing was in view except the empty beach to their right and the dark, empty ocean to their left. After a few minutes Bill said, "Do you think our headlights might be scaring them away?"

"The mobile surveyor was carrying lights. *It* didn't scare them away. And if we turn our lights off, we won't see anything anyway."

"We could switch them off for a few minutes. Maybe some Plutonians will approach in the darkness, and when we turn the lights on again they'll be within reach."

"Try it," Abrams said.

Bill killed the lights and cut the engine. While they sat in the dark he made radio contact again with A Crawler, a hundred miles down the coast. A Crawler had nothing to report. Bill scowled in disappointment. It would be horrible to travel this far and fail to find the Plutonians, he thought. Then he told himself he was being foolish again. They had only just begun to search.

He jabbed at the light control. The brilliant beams blazed forth again.

No Plutonians were in sight. The beach was as empty as before.

"Maybe I didn't give them enough time," Bill said.

"We'll be giving them plenty of time in a little while. It's coming up on bedtime."

"Should we call it a day now?"

"Take us another two miles," Abrams said.

But after a mile Bill decided that they had gone far enough for now. They had been driving for close to nine hours; it had been a fatiguing trip, and this was as good a time as any to knock off for a while. He had the maddening, irrational feeling that they had already gone past the only place on the beach where they stood a chance of finding Plutonians. But they hadn't even come to the point where the mobile surveyor had made its historic discovery.

He brought the crawler to a stop and doused the headlights. They were parked less than twenty feet from the sea, but there was no need to fear that the tide might rise during their period of sleep. There were no tides on this moonless world.

Abrams quickly converted their seats to beds, and they stretched out. Bill allowed himself the luxury of a jolt of sedative from the medicine kit within his suit; he doubted that he'd be able to get to sleep naturally, sealed up in his spacesuit and stiff after so many hours of riding in the crawler. But the drug helped him to slide off into a deep, dreamless sleep, and the dosage kept him under for exactly eight hours.

When he woke, Abrams was already up, but the lights were still off outside the crawler.

"What have I missed?" Bill asked.

"Not a whole lot. I've talked with Commander Spencer —not much going on back at the ship. And I called A Crawler. Pomerantz and Washington haven't found anything yet. They stayed up an hour later than we did. The crawlers are now 96.9 miles from rendezvous point."

"Have you turned on the headlights?"

Abrams shook his head. "I've been waiting for you. But I'll do it now."

He reached for the control. Bill envisioned dozens of Plutonians creeping around outside the ship. Perhaps they all had been gathering while he and Abrams slept—emerging from the sea to inspect the strange object that had parked itself on the beach. And when the headlights went on, they would reveal—

Nothing.

Bill sat blinking in the glare, looking at a beach as empty as it had been before they had gone to sleep. He would have been grateful for the sight of even a single Plutonian scuttling in panic into the sea; but all was still.

This silent world seemed utterly dead.

They studied the screens, hoping that the sonar or one of the other sensors might pick up the image of a Plutonian in motion near the crawler.

Nothing.

They breakfasted and got under way, with Abrams driving, moving at a slow pace toward the south, zigzagging along the beach, now at the very edge of the sea, now a hundred yards inland.

Nothing.

Nothing.

Nothing.

We aren't going to find them, Bill thought.

We aren't going to find a thing.

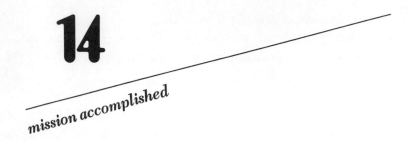

14

mission accomplished

He was wrong, of course.

The Plutonians were discovered when B Crawler was fifty hours out from the ship. By then the exploratory mission had become a thing of grinding dreariness, an unending slow-motion journey down a lifeless beach, broken only by hours of drugged sleep, by drab pre-packaged meals, and by increasingly sparse conversation. The big events were things like the changing of drivers and the hourly call-ins to Commander Spencer at the *Pluto I.* Pluto was not a charming planet. The unvarying bleakness of the landscape, the changelessness of everything, the stillness, the silence—a little of Pluto went a very long way.

But in the fiftieth hour of the journey Bill saw a rock on the beach, deep purple against the icy white.

Abrams was driving. Bill was eyeing the screens in a

dreamy way, having long ago given up any real hope of discovering anything. When he noticed the rock, he checked it off in his mind as a mildly interesting geological feature. The crawler jounced on for another dozen yards while Bill vaguely wondered why it was that he had not seen any other rocks along the beach. The crawler continued ten yards more before it occurred to him that the "rock" might well not be a rock at all.

"Stop!" Bill yelled. "Back up!"

"What's the matter?"

"We just passed a Plutonian!"

There wasn't any doubt about it now. The "rock" had sprouted legs, plenty of them, and was slowly scrabbling up the beach. A second one just like it had emerged from the sea and had paused, resting, just at the shore. A third appeared. A fourth.

Abrams edged the crawler backward until it was only a little way from the group of slow-moving Plutonians. They showed no fear of the vehicle, nor of its bright lights. They were some fifteen feet inland now, close together and moving in an unhurried way toward no particular destination.

"Get the camera moving," Abrams said.

Bill nodded. He jabbed the stud that activated the film mechanism. Abrams, meanwhile, was sending the news to the ship and to A Crawler. Bill felt a sizzling impatience within him; he feared that the alien creatures would scuttle away before they could be caught. But they were making no attempt whatever to flee.

He realized that he wasn't going to have moral qualms about capturing the Plutonians. They hardly looked like beings of any high order of intelligence. Each one was about twice the size of a big man's fist, with small twig-like legs sticking out underneath the thick, heavy-looking, dome-shaped shell. Obviously they hadn't been designed for land travel, since they could just barely haul themselves around on those little stalks of legs; but just as obviously they couldn't be swimming creatures. Bill suspected that they were slow-moving dwellers on the shallow ocean floor, who had some periodic need to venture onto the land. They reminded him more than ever of crabs. But it was a mistake, he realized, to think of them in Earthside terms at all. These were formidably alien beings, utterly different from any life-form of his own planet. He had no way of knowing whether they really did follow the design he had imagined, with silicon-cobalt superconductive bodies and veins that carried liquid Helium II; but their construction, whatever it might be, enabled them to survive at temperatures a few degrees above absolute zero on an airless planet, and that was alien enough.

When they had observed the Plutonians for perhaps five minutes, Bill said, "I think we ought to make the capture now."

"Getting itchy?"

"There'll be plenty of time to study their habits later. I want to make sure we get our specimens while we have the chance."

"Okay: let's get started."

The crawlers had been specially designed for the job of capturing Plutonians. The size of the creatures had been unknown, since the films taken by the mobile surveyor unit had provided no idea of scale, and so the crawlers were prepared to handle anything up to about a ton. A turret at the top of the vehicle housed several kinds of collecting tools, each mounted on a telescoping arm capable of being extended some fifty feet. One was a sort of spoon with a retractable cover, suitable for catching creatures up to a foot in diameter. Another was a metal lasso powered by a winch; another was a huge wire net; another was a great eight-fingered claw.

They tried the claw first. Dave Abrams operated the remote controls of the hunting equipment, and Bill backed the crawler into position. The turret opened and the claw reached out at the end of its long skinny arm. Abrams lowered it over one of the Plutonians; but he was too slow about closing the claw, and the creature, with surprising agility, slithered between two of the metal fingers and escaped. Abrams shook his head. "I was afraid I'd hurt it," he said. "I should have sprung the trap faster."

The Plutonian hadn't gone far away. It had settled on the ice a dozen feet from the hovering claw. Abrams raised the claw again, brought it down, snapped it shut—

—and failed again. The claw was simply too big; the Plutonian was able to tumble through the space between fingers.

"Try the spoon," Bill suggested.

The spoon was more useful. Abrams maneuvered it toward one of the Plutonians, brought it down to ground level, and scooped up the Plutonian and an inch-deep layer of the ice underneath it. A touch of a knob and the spoon's cover moved into place, trapping the Plutonian within. Now Abrams swung the arm back toward the crawler. A collecting tank with a capacity of about a hundred cubic feet was mounted at the crawler's rear; Abrams lowered the spoon into the tank, retracted the cover, let the Plutonian crawl off the spoon. "Do you think he can get out of there?" Abrams asked.

"I doubt it. But I'll keep an eye on him."

Bill monitored the scene in the collecting tank while Abrams sent the spoon after a second Plutonian. The captured specimen was creeping slowly about on the floor of the tank, displaying very little curiosity about its new surroundings. Glancing at the adjoining screen, Bill saw Abrams slide the spoon under another of the creatures, close the cover, and swing the arm toward the collecting tank.

In a little while five Plutonians were moving to and fro in the tank. "That's about enough, isn't it?" Abrams asked.

"I think so. Now we'd better give them some refreshment."

He backed the crawler around so that Abrams could reach the sea with the spoon-arm. Abrams began to scoop up the liquid methane and pour it into the tank. In ten minutes there was a foot-deep pool of methane in the tank to keep the Plutonians moist. Just in case they needed to come above the surface frequently, Abrams broke loose a chunk of ice with the claw and carefully inserted it in the tank as a perch. The last step was to slide a wire-mesh cover over the tank to keep the Plutonians from clambering out.

"Mission accomplished," Abrams said. "Let's get going."

Bill drove. Abrams notified the ship of their success, and then called down to A Crawler. Lou Pomerantz congratulated them a little ruefully; he and Washington hadn't seen a thing but icy desolation so far.

"Spencer wants us to proceed to rendezvous point as

originally planned," Abrams said. "After we've met we can head back to the ship in convoy."

"Check. Marty makes our position out as about 30.3 miles due south of yours."

"That matches," said Abrams. "Now that we've got some Plutonians, we can push the speed up a little. Say, fifteen mph—that should bring us together in about an hour."

B Crawler moved steadily southward. Twice Bill caught sight of other Plutonians: a group of three emerging from the sea, and then a pair, heading back from the land. So they weren't really uncommon, then. It had just been a matter of bad timing or bad luck that had kept the Plutonians out of sight during the first two days of the journey.

He watched the five captives in the collecting tank closely. What worried him was that they might be suffering or dying in there. He knew nothing about the living habits of the Plutonians; possibly confinement in the same close quarters for more than a few minutes would be fatal. The Plutonians didn't look bothered at all; they continued to move in slow circles around the floor of the tank, occasionally clambering ponderously up on their lump of ice for a few moments. But Bill was troubled enough so that after half an hour he had Abrams halt the crawler, empty all the methane from the tank, and scoop in a fresh supply from the sea. Then they continued on to the rendezvous point, halfway between the points at which the two crawlers had begun their trek along the coast.

There was no sign of A Crawler.

When fifteen minutes had gone by, Bill said, "They must have stopped to make a catch."

"No doubt," Dave Abrams agreed.

But fifteen minutes later, A Crawler still had not appeared. The occupants of B Crawler were exchanging worried glances. Pomerantz and Washington were half an hour overdue, and there was no comforting explanation for it.

"Call them," Bill said.

Abrams reached for the phones as though he had simply been waiting for Bill to suggest it. He punched for the channel to A Crawler and told them to come in.

No answer.

"Do you read me, A? Come in, A! A, are you reading me?"

Silence.

"Something wrong with their transmitter?" Bill asked. "Maybe a breakdown on account of the cold?"

Abrams scowled at the communications equipment. He shouted into the phones; but all was quiet at the other end. With a brusque gesture he switched to the ship channel. "Come in, *Pluto I*, come in, come in!" he snapped tensely.

"*Pluto I*," a voice replied. "Santell here. Who's this?"

"Abrams and Hastings, in B Crawler. Where's Spencer?"

"Went to sleep ten minutes ago," the geophysicist said. "Right after you called in the news about the Plutonians."

"You help me, then. When did you last hear from A Crawler?"

"At the last call-in time. Maybe forty minutes ago. Why?"

"I can't pick them up on my phones."

"Hold it," Santell said. "I'll check the surveillance

equipment." There was a long silence. Then he said, "I've located them on the screen. Their position is—umm—nine or ten miles due south of yours, near the coast."

"Are they moving?"

"No," Santell said. "The dot's holding still on the screen."

"Call them. I'll hold."

An endless time went by. Bill peered studiously at the Plutonians in the tank and tried hard not to think of the possible troubles that A Crawler might be in. Neither he nor Abrams said anything.

Finally Santell's voice returned. "They don't answer my signal. And there's some odd stuff on one of the screens here—the *malfunction* light is on, but I don't know what's being monitored on that screen. Maybe the condition of the crawler itself. Yes, that must be it: something's wrong with the crawler."

"Can you find the screen that's reporting spacesuit telemetry?" Abrams asked urgently. "At least we'll know if they're still alive."

Santell hesitated. "I'm not sure. There's so much surveillance stuff here—"

"Wake up Spencer, then!"

"Can't. He's out on an eight-hour drug jolt. I'll have to do the best I can without him. Let's see—fuel, internal temperature, pressure—whoops!"

"What is it?"

"I'm getting an impossible reading for A Crawler's temperature and pressure levels. They're both level with the external atmosphere. What does that mean?"

"Maybe that the crawler fell down a crevasse and split open," Abrams said. "Or maybe just that Washington and

Pomerantz decided to take a stroll. *Find the spacesuit readings!*"

"I'm trying, Dave, I'm trying. You've got to remember that I'm just filling in while Spencer's asleep. I don't really know what all this stuff is supposed to—ah—here. Yes. Yes. They're okay, Dave. Spacesuit readings all normal, pressure, temperature, everything. Both of them."

Abrams let out a low whistle of relief. "All right. Look, I'm going to drive down the coast and see what's going on. Keep the communications circuit open and clue me in on their position as I get near them. If you happen to hear anything from them, let me know right away."

"Will do," Santell said.

Abrams broke contact and started the crawler. Soon he had it up to top speed. The Plutonians didn't care much for that, evidently; Bill could see them paddling around in the churning methane of their tank.

"What do you think the trouble really is?" he asked.

Abrams shrugged. "I don't even want to think about it. But we'll know soon enough. Even if their crawler has conked out, we ought to be within reach of their suit radios in another mile. Those things have a range of seven or eight miles in this kind of atmosphere, I guess."

He began trying the frequency of Pomerantz and Washington's suit radios when B Crawler was eight miles from the indicated position of the other vehicle. But nothing except static came through for the first few minutes. Then Lou Pomerantz could be heard to say, "—darkest place I ever saw."

"Where are you, Lou?"

"That you, Dave?"

"Yeah. We're heading toward you. What happened?"

"The ground opened up and swallowed us."

"Huh?"

"A crevasse appeared out of nowhere. Some kind of underground shift, I don't know—the sonar didn't give any warning. All of a sudden we were falling down a hole. Just like Alice, but I didn't see the White Rabbit."

"You're okay, though?"

"I am," Pomerantz said. "I don't know about Marty Washington. He isn't saying anything, and I can't reach him."

"Can't reach him? What's your situation, anyway?"

"The crawler cracked open when we hit bottom. We're —oh, maybe a hundred feet down, and we hit hard. We got dumped out with the wreckage of the crawler between us. There's probably jagged metal all over the place, and I don't dare try to climb over to see how Marty is. One rip in my suit and it's bye-bye for Louie. I'm just sitting here in the dark wondering how long it's going to be before the ice gives another shrug and the crevasse closes up again."

"Just sit tight. We'll be there in two minutes."

"You better be!"

"We will," Abrams said. "And don't worry about Marty. Maybe he got knocked cold, but he's still okay. He's tele-metering normal data back to the ship."

"Good deal. Hurry up and pull us out, now!"

Abrams switched to the ship channel. "You hear all that?"

"I've been listening," said Santell. "What are you going to do?"

"Pull them up with our collecting arms. You wake Spencer up yet?"

"He's deep under."

"Okay, we'll have to work things out without consulting him. What's our indicated position relative to A Crawler?"

"Less than a mile. The dots are getting so close I can't give you anything better than that."

"Good enough. We ought to pick up their crevasse on the sonar pretty soon."

"There it is now," Bill said.

Abrams nodded. "Right. It's a thousand yards ahead. We'll have them out of there in no time."

"Be careful," Santell warned. "If the ice is unstable, you may be in danger yourselves."

"Can't worry about that now," Abrams said. "Let's just figure we've had all the lousy luck we're going to have."

He inched the crawler toward the crevasse. In a few moments they were close enough to see the deadly trap on their screens: a dark gash splitting the brightness of the icefield at right angles to the shoreline. Abrams braked the crawler when they were less than fifty feet away.

"Make sure your spacesuit's sealed," he said. "Here's where we say good-bye to our atmosphere."

They both ran through a quick spacesuit check. Then Abrams opened the hatch and they climbed out of the crawler. It was the first chance they had had to stretch their legs in more than two days, and Bill could feel every muscle creaking. Abrams grabbed a portable searchlight and they walked together to the edge of the abyss. The ice seemed firm enough, right up to the rim.

But it was dizzying to peer over. Abrams leaned far out and let the beam shine into the crevasse. It was perhaps forty feet wide at the top, but its sides sloped sharply in a V. The shattered crawler was wedged lengthwise close to the bottom, well over a hundred feet down. One spacesuited figure lay to each side of the vehicle on the floor of the crevasse.

Abrams grunted in displeasure. "Deep," he said. "Too deep for our collecting arms. But we'll manage. Hey, Lou, do you read me!"

"You're coming through beautifully," Pomerantz said. "How do things look?"

"Not bad, not good. We'll work something out in a minute." Abrams motioned Bill back from the brink and said, "This is going to be tricky, but we ought to make it. What we'll do is bring our crawler a little closer to the edge—another ten, twenty feet shouldn't be too risky. Then we take our hundred-foot rope and tie it to the end of one of the collecting arms. We lower the arm into the crevasse and let the rope dangle down to them. Lou crawls over to Marty, ties the rope around him, and we reel him in. Then we pull up Lou. Simple?"

"If the rope reaches," Bill said.

"It'll reach," said Abrams.

But it didn't. They got it from the supply cabinet—a good sturdy strand of superfine cable, guaranteed to remain flexible even at these temperatures—and fastened it securely to the winch-powered arm that terminated in a lasso. That was the arm capable of bearing the greatest weight. Abrams extended the arm to its fullest range and Bill guided the attached rope into the crevasse. He was dismayed to see that it dangled far above Lou Pomerantz' head.

He gestured Abrams to bring the crawler closer to the

edge of the crevasse. Abrams came forward twenty feet, right to the limit of any sensible safety margin. The rope still fell short. Bill beckoned again, and again the crawler came closer.

And closer. And closer. At last it stood with its front treads only a yard from the edge. The ice seemed to be creaking and groaning under the weight. Abrams got out and inspected the situation. The end of the rope hung a good four feet above Lou Pomerantz' straining hands.

"Do we have more rope?" Bill asked.

"No. And we can't get the crawler much closer to the edge. Another foot, maybe, tops. Which isn't good enough."

"What do we do? Ask Santell to drive out here with the spare crawler and a longer line?"

"We can't wait that long. He'd need half a day to get here, and that crevasse might close again any minute. But there's another way—not easy, but we can try."

"Go ahead."

Abrams said, "We unfasten the line from the collecting arm. I tie the lasso around my legs and you lower me into the abyss, holding the line in my hands. If I dangle head downward, it'll make up that last gap of four or five feet to Pomerantz. It means I'll get an awful headache, but it shouldn't take more than a minute or so for him to tie the line to Marty's suit and for you to haul me up. How does it sound?"

"Brilliant," Bill said. "I've got only one slight change to suggest."

"What?"

"I do the acrobatic dangling and you operate the machinery."

"Quit it, Bill. I'm military personnel. If there's any difficult or dangerous work, I'm the one in this team who's going to be doing it. If that crevasse closes up while you're in it—"

"I'll be squashed flat," Bill said. "Just as flat as you'd be if you were the one who went down. And I guess my mother would cry and the President would send my folks a medal. But you have a wife and two children who'd like to see you come back alive. I'm an eighteen-year-old bachelor who isn't all that important to any other people."

"You're wasting time, Bill. I'm going down there, and you're not going to take any risks that are meant for me. This is my job. Get in the crawler and start lowering the arm."

"If you go down," Bill said evenly, "you better figure out some way of operating the arm too. I'm not going to do it for you."

"But—"

"And you're wasting time, Dave. That crevasse might close up while we stand here arguing. Get into the crawler!"

"I order you to operate the arm," Abrams said.

"I'm a civilian, remember? I'm not taking your orders, and you're not going to make me sit in that crawler while the father of two kids risks his life. Go on, Dave. I mean it."

Abrams stared at him for a long moment. He shook his head and muttered, "This is a miserable thing for you to do, Bill. It's my responsibility to go down there."

"It's your responsibility to operate the arm. You've been trained to use it. I've never touched the controls in my life. I'd rather take my chances in the crevasse than to run machinery I don't understand while someone else's life is at stake."

Abrams was silent. Bill realized he had hit on the right line of argument at last: it wasn't a matter of heroism, it was a matter of experience. He had to be the one to go down, because Abrams had to run the equipment. Abrams seemed to realize the logic of it. "All right," he muttered. "You win."

He turned and trudged across the ice, got into the crawler, went to the controls. The lasso arm and line came up from the abyss. Bill unfastened the line and secured the lasso about his ankles, pulling the metal cord in as tightly as he dared. Then he waved to Abrams.

The lasso arm rose in the air and moved out over the crevasse, with Bill hanging from it. In his right hand he gripped the line and in his left he held the searchlight. Carefully Abrams lowered him into the yawning crack in ice—twenty, thirty, forty feet down, until the telescoping arm was at its full length. Bill aimed the light at the floor of the crevasse and radioed down to Pomerantz, "You've got room to creep under the crawler, don't you, Lou? Looks to me like it's edged about eight feet off the bottom. Go underneath it and over to Marty. Then I'll drop you the line."

"Right," Pomerantz said.

With infinite care he began to move on hands and knees along the crevasse floor. Not much light was reaching him down there, and the danger of snagging his plastic spacesuit on some sharp jutting corner of the wrecked crawler was great. Bill held his breath and watched tautly as Pomerantz vanished under the bulk of the wreckage, was hidden a long while, and emerged finally on the far side next to Marty Washington.

"How is he?" Bill asked.

"Out cold, but his suit's still functioning. I think he'll be okay."

Now came the most difficult part of the maneuver. Bill clipped the searchlight to his suit belt to leave both his hands free, let go of the collecting arm, and slowly let himself descend until he was hanging head downward like a trapeze artist with the lasso gripping his ankles.

Pluto's extra-heavy gravity brought a dizzying rush of blood to his brain. For one terrible moment he thought he was going to lose consciousness; but he nudged the chin controls of his suit to feed him extra oxygen, and forced himself to stay alert. He knotted one end of the hundred-foot line about his wrists and let the other end fall toward the men below.

Would it be long enough?

Yes! Lou Pomerantz caught it and held it up, grinning. While Bill dangled, Pomerantz slipped the rope through the belt-loop of Marty Washington's spacesuit and tied it securely.

"All set," he said. "Heave!"

Dave Abrams, listening over the suit-radio channel from the cabin of the crawler, switched on the winch of the collecting arm. The arm began to rise—and Bill thought his own arms and legs both would rip from their sockets. He was the weakest link in the chain of rescue, for the collecting arm to which he was tied and the line that was tied to him both were of uncomplaining metal, and he was fashioned from flesh that had hardly been designed for this kind of treatment. Numb, dazed, he swung like a pendulum in the crevasse, now approaching this side and now that side of the glassy-walled cleft. At any moment the ground might shift and the crevasse snap shut on the three of them like a monstrous mouth. Unless his arms came off first.

Up—up—up—

Suddenly he was over the edge of the crevasse and sprawling on the ice while the collecting arm continued to reel itself in. In another moment Marty Washington appeared. Bill felt his head clearing; he got his legs free of the lasso, ran to the unconscious man, and pulled him safely clear of the abyss. Then he radioed to Abrams, "All right, I'm going to go back down for Pomerantz now."

"You must be bushed. Let me go down."

"Don't start that again," Bill said. He was already fastening the lasso about his legs. "Up we go!"

Abrams lifted him, and for the second time Bill began the descent into the abyss. It went more quickly this time, since there was no need to wait while the rope was tied to an unconscious man. Bill swung to the head-down position and extended the line to Pomerantz, who made it secure, and they began to rise. Once again Bill carried another man's entire weight in the most uncomfortable possible way; once again he felt his brain flooding with blood, and was buffeted by confusions and delusions bordering on hallucination; once more he thought his limbs would split apart. But it was only a matter of moments before the winch had hoisted both of them out of the abyss. Bill touched solid ground alongside the crawler, freed his legs, stood up, and promptly caved in. He clung to the ice while all the universe spiraled wildly about him.

The spasm of dizziness passed. He sat up groggily and

looked around. Marty Washington had returned to consciousness and stood not far from him. Lou Pomerantz was disengaging himself from the rescue line. Dave Abrams was pulling the crawler away from its dangerous position by the rim of the crevasse.

"We missed the sunrise while we were down in that hole," Pomerantz said.

"Sunrise? What sunrise?" Bill asked.

"Look up there."

Bill turned. The sky looked vastly altered, now, for into it had come a star that had not been there an hour ago, a star whose cold radiance was hundreds of times as bright as that of the full moon seen from Earth. Brilliant as the star was, it was impossible to recognize it as the familiar yellow sun. But its frosty light sent glittering tracks of dazzling brightness along the forlorn icefields of Pluto. Suddenly the men on the ice had shadows. Suddenly the blackness of the sky was tinged with green as the distant sunlight bounced through Pluto's faint atmosphere. Suddenly this dreadful planet was transformed.

Sunrise. Sunrise on Pluto.

Bill half expected to hear the birds of morning singing in the trees.

"That explains the crevasse," Marty Washington said. "Dawn was coming up—the temperature must have been rising by a couple of degrees. Enough to get the ice in motion."

"It ought to get us in motion too," Lou Pomerantz said. "This whole coastal region may start cracking up as the morning goes along."

Washington laughed. "If we fall in again, old Bill will pull us out again."

"Sure," Bill said. "Shucks, nothing to it!"

"And if Bill falls in with us?" Pomerantz asked.

They laughed and walked a little more quickly toward the crawler, which had come to rest about a hundred yards away. Abruptly Bill felt the ground lurch beneath his feet. He fell forward, thinking as he dropped that he must be getting another fit of the dizzies; but he saw Lou and Marty topple also, and realized it was some upheaval of the ice under the strain of the rising temperature. Even the slight additional warmth provided by the incredibly remote sun was enough to disturb the equilibrium of forces, this close to absolute zero.

After a moment all grew still again. Bill rose uncertainly, steadied himself, looked around.

The crevasse was gone. Only a rough upraised ridge of broken ice marked the place where it had been.

They stared in awe at the sight.

"Close one," Lou Pomerantz muttered. "We don't need them any closer."

They ran for the crawler. Dave Abrams helped them in. Bill went last, for it had occurred to him that, as long as he was out in the open, he had a chance to take a close look at the Plutonians. He peered into the collecting tank. The five glossy domes were perambulating as placidly as ever, displaying no visible enthusiasm over the Plutonian sunrise. Bill was unable to make out any details of their bodies; he saw neither eyes nor mouths under the edges of the thick shells, only legs that seemed to sprout from the shell surface itself. It was going to be a problem, he realized, to carry out any sort of analysis of creatures that had to be kept at such low temperatures. The job called for xenobiologists in spacesuits; it would be even

230

more cumbersome than working with the Old Martians.

"You waiting for the next crevasse?" Lou Pomerantz called.

Bill hurried into the crawler. If it had been cramped in there when just he and Dave Abrams had occupied it, it was impossibly scrambled now. And all four of them would have to keep their spacesuits on for the rest of the trip, since the atmosphere in the crawler now was that of Pluto.

Abrams keyed in the accelerator. Moving at its top speed, B Crawler set out on the five-hour journey to the ship.

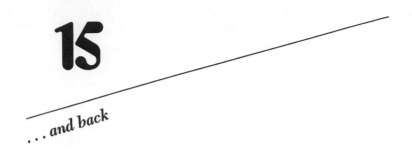

15

...and back

Loading the Plutonians aboard the *Pluto I* was a slow job. One of the fore cabins had been designed as a receiving tank, refrigerated to Plutonian tastes and sealed to prevent atmospheric mingling. It had been pumped full of the chilly hydrogen-helium mixture that passed for air on Pluto, and it was awash with liquid methane and lumps of frozen-ammonia ice. In all respects the receiving tank was a miniature duplicate of Pluto, in which the five captives ought to be perfectly comfortable on the voyage to the World's Fair. The only difficulty was getting them into the ship without exposing them to the environment of Earthmen.

That meant replacing the wire top of the collecting tank with a sealed lid—which took half a day—and hoisting the whole tank into the ship. Then it was necessary

232

to dolly the tank through a narrow corridor to the receiving tank. With immense care the collecting tank and the receiving tank had to be lined up so that one would open into the other, while avoiding atmospheric contamination. It was possible to get the two tanks open by using the pair of remote-control handling arms mounted within the receiving tank; but getting the Plutonians to cross from one tank to the other exhausted everybody's patience.

The Plutonians showed no real interest in going anywhere. They seemed quite content to remain in the first tank. The handling arms of the receiving tank were able to reach only a short distance into the collecting tank, not far enough actually to grab any of the Plutonians; about the best that could be done was to wave the tips of the arms around in the hope that the Plutonians would be attracted by the motion and would go into the larger tank.

They weren't—not at first. It took them a long time to react at all to the moving objects that were sticking into their tank, and when they did notice them their response was to move away, solemnly creeping to the far side of their tank, where they piled up on a chunk of ice like so many turtles basking in the sun. There they stayed for three hours, hardly moving at all. Lou Pomerantz and Bill took turns operating the handling arms in a spirit of growing futility; they sat for an hour at a stretch apiece with their own hands thrust into the controls of the handlers, wiggling their fingers in what they hoped would be a seductive motion. Nothing much happened. Finally Bill had the inspiration of breaking off a small chunk of ammonia ice and waving it about with one of the handlers. He waved it for fifteen minutes; then one of the Plutonians took heed and timidly paddled over to inspect it. Bill pulled the handler back toward the receiving tank, and the Plutonian, its dim curiosity aroused, followed. Ten minutes more and a second Plutonian had come across. The third followed swiftly enough, but the fourth required an hour of coaxing, and the fifth half an hour more.

At last the receiving tank was sealed. An hour later, *Pluto I* lifted off for the homeward trip.

The expedition had been a total success on its own terms. Pluto had been explored to some extent with only one mishap and no loss of life; specimens of native life had been taken alive; preliminary geophysical studies had been carried out; some astronomical work had begun to answer a few of the questions about the eccentricity of Pluto's orbit. It was only a beginning—a very skimpy beginning—but at no time had this been intended as a major scientific reconnaissance of the ninth planet. It had been—and there was no getting away from it—mainly a publicity stunt for the benefit of Claude Regan's World's Fair.

Bill no longer minded that. He had traveled far; he had seen wonders; he had taken part in an unforgettable exploit. He was even a hero of sorts after the crevasse rescue.

"How does it feel, being a hero?" Lou Pomerantz asked him, when they were three days out from Pluto and streaking along at several million miles an hour.

Bill shrugged. "I guess it'll give me a lively chapter for my memoirs."

"And me for mine! Boy, when I saw you hanging by your heels in the middle of the air, I told myself that this was one stunt that wasn't going to work: I figured you'd come loose and land on the bottom with Marty and me."

"I would have left my legs behind, then," Bill said. "That lasso doesn't let go easily."

"And when the crevasse closed up five minutes after you got us out—" Pomerantz shuddered. "What a story that's going to make!"

Bill felt a little glum about that. He knew there was going to be tremendous public interest in their exploits on Pluto; he was going to have to tell the crevasse story over and over again, adopting the kind of aw-gee modesty that was expected from heroes, until he was thoroughly sick of the whole thing. He hadn't been thinking much about heroism when he had insisted on being the one to enter the crevasse. It was just something unpleasant that had to be done, and done fast, and he had done it. Now he would have to live with it forever. Bill Hastings, Boy Hero: that wasn't his style at all. He could imagine the tridim that Hollywood would soon be making, with somebody incredibly brawny and handsome playing the Bill Hastings role, and the scene at the crevasse turned into something infinitely harrowing and agonizing, with plenty of loud screeching discordant music and close-up shots of sweating foreheads behind spacesuit viewplates. They would exaggerate the incident until it began to look like the thirteenth labor of Hercules, and for the rest of his life people would think of him in Hollywood terms.

I don't want to be Bill Hastings, Boy Hero, he told himself. I just want to be a xenobiologist, doing my research and going on expeditions and maybe helping to discover something important.

Despite himself, he had to admit that the crevasse business was likely to improve his standing in Emily Blackman's eyes. Being a tridim hero wasn't so bad so far as that was concerned. It would give him just that extra touch of glamor that he needed for membership in the sort of society Emily inhabited.

The eye of his mind projected a scene for him: the day of his return to the World's Fair, as he stepped triumphantly from the *Pluto I* to be met by a handshake and a grateful clap on the back from Claude Regan—and there was Emily, waving to him, tears in her eyes, all her cool sophistication vanished now in her joy at his safe return. "I'm so glad you're back," she would whisper. "I was terribly worried about you . . . and it was such a wonderful thing, when you pulled those two men out of the crevasse. . . ."

It made a nice romantic image.

When he wasn't allowing himself the luxury of daydreams of this sort, Bill spent his time studying the Plutonians via closed-circuit video, though the ship wasn't really equipped for much in the way of xenobiological research. The best he could do under the circumstances was monitor the Plutonians' environment in an attempt to see what nutrients they might be drawing from their atmosphere and the liquid methane. But it was impossible to discover anything significant. Real research would have to wait until the Plutonians were installed in a real laboratory.

One thing seemed certain, though: there wasn't going to be much work for xenolinguists or xenopsychologists. Biologically the Plutonians were fascinating; but they were primitive creatures, sluggish and unintelligent, totally lacking in the charm and complexity of the Old Martians. That was no real surprise. For life to exist at all at the borders of absolute zero was amazing; for intelligent life to have evolved under such awesomely difficult conditions was beyond probability. Nobody was going to give these Plutonians nicknames, and no one was going to regard them as individual beings.

"Which is no drawback at all," Bill said. "If we don't have to look upon the Plutonians as people in their own right, we won't get into all the ethical debates that came up over the Old Martians."

Lou Pomerantz grinned slyly. "Meaning that we can do as we please with the Plutonians, in the name of science?"

"Well—"

"Dissect them alive, or anything else?"

"Well, as long as we've only got five of them, it would be wrong to kill any of them, but—"

"Forget that there are only five. How are we going to find out what makes life work on Pluto if we don't open some of them up?"

"We've never dissected an Old Martian, though," Bill said uncomfortably.

"Because we regard them as intelligent beings with individual rights. But these are just purple crabs, more or less. With an extraordinary metabolic system that we don't comprehend at all. Wouldn't you say, therefore, that it's morally justifiable to dissect some of them for the sake of increasing scientific knowledge?"

"We don't know that they aren't intelligent," Bill said. "I mean, they may be cleverer than they look. Maybe they communicate by telepathy and have a rich and intricate culture and—"

"Do you really think so?"

"No, but at least it's possible. And if we took one and

opened it up, and—" Bill hesitated. "Lou, why did you lead me into this discussion?"

Laughing, Pomerantz said, "To show you that it can be just as complicated arriving at an ethical position toward Plutonians as it is toward Old Martians. You've picked a tough science, Bill. Now that mankind is going to other worlds, stumbling unexpectedly over alien creatures, trying to define their rights and status, it's going to be one philosophical headache after another. The Old Martians are treated as people because they talk and think and even look vaguely human. Even so, we kidnapped six of them to be sideshow freaks. Now we've got Plutonians who are so unimaginably alien that we don't know what to make of them, and we've kidnapped some of those, too, but the question is, do we regard them as the low form of life they seem to be, or do we treat them with the repect due the citizens of another world? Are they weird crabs or are they people?"

"I imagine we'll do some dissecting," Bill said, "and regard them as low-order creatures until we learn otherwise."

"I imagine so too. There's so much to learn from a life form that lives at those temperatures that we'd *have* to study it in the greatest possible detail. But you see the problem, don't you? And who knows what we'll find if we ever land on Jupiter or Saturn or Uranus?"

Bill nodded. Last year, dwelling Earthside and daydreaming about becoming a xenobiologist, he had not even begun to consider the complexities of man's relation to alien beings. Now he had a wider sense of the philosophical difficulties ahead, as humanity's boundaries were extended toward the stars. Already the Old Martians had their passionate defenders against man's insatiable curiosity. Would there be a Society for the Prevention of Cruelty to Plutonians? Would a whole new branch of law come into being to protect the rights of alien beings? What would it be called, he wondered—xenojurisprudence?

Life was complicated enough, Bill thought, when we had only one planet to worry about.

He and Lou reached no conclusions in their discussion. It was too early to come by any answers; they were just beginning to discover the questions. Most xenobiologists, Bill now saw, were troubled by feelings of guilt, and yet they went right on prying into the secrets of the beings they studied. He suspected that he would have the same double-faced attitude when he began his own work.

Early in April the journey of the *Pluto I* came to its end.

Two uneventful weeks in space had brought the ship back to the World's Fair Satellite. It matched orbits with the Fair, hovering alongside. The first order of business was to transfer the Plutonians to the pavilion that had been built to house them. After a good many hours of coaxing, the aliens had been persuaded to return to the collecting tank; the sealed tank was dollied up to the hatch of the ship and turned over to spacesuit-clad technicians, who carried it across to a waiting shuttle. The shuttle towed it to the Fair Satellite, where Dr. Martinson and the other xenobiologists waited eagerly to receive it. Before long the Plutonians were wandering about in their new home—an immense cubical tank that duplicated, as closely as possible, the conditions of atmosphere, temperature, and pressure found on their native world.

While this was going on, the explorers were going through an elaborate ceremony of welcome.

Claude Regan was there, shaking everyone's hand just as Bill had imagined, and a kind of controlled pandemonium prevailed as the seven voyagers boarded the Fair Satellite, were duly presented to selected representatives of the news media, were allowed to say a word or two into the microphones, listened to the congratulations of assorted diplomats and high officials, and—after a parade past the Hall of the Worlds, the Global Factors Pavilion, the Mars Pavilion, and the new Pluto Pavilion—were taken away for rest, debriefing, and hearty dinner in privacy.

Bill had tolerated all the noise and uproar of the welcoming; he had expected it to happen just that way, and he was prepared. But one thing troubled him. He saw no sign of Emily.

He hadn't exactly thought that she would rush up and throw her arms about him in front of everyone. But he couldn't even see her in the cheering crowds, though he saw plenty of other members of the Fair staff. During the endless speeches his eyes kept roving up one row and down the next, searching faces . . . and not finding hers.

After dinner came another formal event at the Hall of the Worlds: a special reception for relatives of the voyagers. The seven from the *Pluto I* entered the hall to see a milling throng that resolved itself into wives, parents, brothers, sisters.

"Mom!" Bill cried in amazement. "Dad!" And there was his brother. And his sister with her new husband beside her. They rushed upon him.

"So proud of you—"

"My baby—"

"Was it really cold there, Bill?—"

"What was it like traveling so fast?"

"The people on Pluto—"

"We worried so much—"

"Tell us all about—"

"When you pulled them out of—"

"Was it scary?"

"We read about you every day—"

They were all talking at once, babbling in their happiness. It took him ten minutes to calm them down. His mother, of course, hadn't wanted to come to the Fair; but Claude Regan himself had called and persuaded her to come, saying that it wouldn't be right for a hero not to be welcomed back by all his family. And here they were.

It was a fine moment, but a little exhausting.

Afterward came the press conference, which was ten times as strenuous as dangling in the crevasse had been. And still later—*much* later—the Pluto heroes were allowed to stagger off to get some rest. In the morning there would be more interviews, more celebrations, more excitement.

At least he could be alone for a while, first. He sank down gratefully on the bed in the elegant room they had given him in the Fair's fanciest hotel. But he was wide awake, and he found no pleasure in being alone. He stared for a while at the telephone; and then he started to punch the number of Emily's dorm room. Some mysterious impulse led him to stop midway. He cancelled the call and punched the number of the room where he had bunked before everything had started to happen.

Mel Salter's plump face appeared on the screen.

"Hi," Bill said. "I wake you up?"

"Nope. Where'd they put you?"

"Galactic Hotel. But I suppose I'll be moving back to the old place when the fuss dies down."

Mel grinned. "Don't you think you rate something fancier now?"

"All I want is a place to hit the pillow," Bill said.

They talked for a little while about the expedition. It was a lame, halting conversation; Mel seemed ill at ease, as though the weeks Bill had been away had erected a barrier of some sort between them. He seemed to regard Bill now as a being too famous for mere chatter, and half a dozen times they fell into silence that Bill had to break with an effort.

He said, "And how's the Fair been going? Financially, I mean."

"It's in great shape," Mel said. "Sold out through the end of the year. Soon as news broke that you were on your way back with Plutonians, that did it."

"Regan's gamble paid off, then."

"Sure did."

There was another sticky silence.

Bill decided it was time to bring the talk around to important matters. He said, "I sort of thought I'd hear from Emily tonight."

"Emily." Mel repeated the name in a curiously flat way.

"Emily, yes. Your cousin Emily Blackman. You remember her?"

"Yes. Emily. Well, look, Bill—I mean—that is—"

Salter fell into embarrassed incoherence.

"What is it?" Bill shouted. "What's happened to her?"

"Nothing's happened, exactly. Not yet, that is. But—"

"*Where is she?*"

"She went back to Earth last week," Mel blurted.

"To Earth? Is she sick?"

"Well, no." Mel tugged at one fleshy earlobe. "Listen, Bill, this is kind of awkward. But she left a message for you. I'll send it over by tube, okay? It'll give you the whole story." He looked so unhappy that Bill let him break the contact. Then he waited an intolerable ten minutes while the message from Emily made its way through the pneumatic tube network that connected the buildings of the Fair. He tried to guess what might have happened. Illness in her family? Had the Blackmans lost all their money and been forced to call her home? Was it some sort of nervous breakdown?

The message arrived. With fumbling fingers he slipped it into the playback slot of his room phone, and Emily's features appeared on the screen. She stared straight out at him, dark eyes sparkling.

"Bill, love, you'll get this when you come back from Pluto, and before I say anything else, I want to tell you how happy I am for you that you were able to go there and do all the wonderful things that you've been doing. I haven't missed one newsflash about the expedition. It's been grand knowing someone as brave and as important as you, and I expect to tell all my grandchildren that I was right there when you were starting your terrific career.

"Now for my news. I won't be able to be there to welcome you back, because I'm going to Earth tomorrow. Nick and I have decided to get married in June. I know it sounds sort of sudden, but it really isn't, because the Antonellis and the Blackmans have been friends for a million years, and Nick and I have known each other since we were kids, and we more or less assumed that we'd get married one of these days. And the other night we realized that it was going to be this year.

"So we'll be on Earth when you come back to the Fair. In my family a wedding is a big thing, and I've got ten billion things to do between now and June, so I can't wait for your return even though I know I really ought to. Maybe if you aren't too busy with your Martians and your Plutonians and everything you'll take a few days off and come down to Earth for our wedding. If you can't make it, we'll see you before long anyway, because we'll be honeymooning on Mars and plan to stop off at the Fair first to visit the Plutonians. And you.

"That's about the whole scoop, Bill. I just want to say how glad I was to have known you, and how much I hope we'll go on being friends later on. And I hope you'll forgive me for some of the nasty things I said and did. There are times I hate myself for being like that. But everyone says that marriage will mellow me, and maybe it will. So long, Bill. Be seeing you soon."

She winked and blew him a kiss and the tape ended.

Bill played the message through four times in a row without pausing. By then it had begun to sink in.

Emily.

Marrying.

Nick.

He was stunned and shaken, but yet he couldn't say he was altogether surprised. There had always seemed to be something going on between those two.

And he couldn't pretend to himself that he had had any claim on Emily himself. She had put it accurately enough in her message: they had just been friends. Everything else had been entirely in his imagination. He didn't belong in her world, and she wasn't part of his. She would go on to a career of dinner parties and holidays in expensive resorts and friendships with the great ones of politics and finance, and he would spend his days in laboratories and his travel time on field trips to distant worlds. Not all his heroism nor all the glamor of having been to Pluto would ever allow him to feel comfortable in her circle of moneyed socialites.

He forced a grin. Welcome back to reality, Boy Hero! This is the way the world works. It isn't all like a tridim script. You win the essay contest, you go to the World's Fair, and even get to Pluto and become famous—but you don't necessarily wind up with the beautiful rich girl at the end.

Somehow he didn't want to be alone just now. He dressed and slipped out of the room, and made his way from the hotel by the back way, in case any reporters were lurking in the lobby. He emerged in a quiet street of the Fair and headed for the uplevel ramp. His destination was Overlevel Five, where the Mars and Pluto pavilions were located.

Some of the pain of Emily's message ebbed from him as he strode through the Fair. He knew he'd recover: his little dream had never been very real to him, and so he wouldn't suffer long from its rude ending. Besides, he was soon going to be too busy to worry about such things.

Reality was setting in again, he saw. His Pluto adventure was over, and in a few days the celebrations would be finished; he would be one of yesterday's heroes, just a name in the history books. And then he could get down to the important business at hand. First, to get through the five months that still remained of his prize year at the Fair. Then college. Then graduate work. And then his career.

He wished it were September now. He had been at the World's Fair long enough, and the excitement of its gaiety no longer mattered to him. He was ready to go home and begin to learn. There was so much for him to learn before he could hope to go to space again! These past few months he had been playing a little game, pretending he was a xenobiologist, and it had been fun; but winning an essay contest was no substitute for a solid scientific education. If he wanted to do real research, he'd have to put in many long Earthbound years of study.

And then—

Well, there was a whole universe waiting for him.

He got off the ramp at Overlevel Five and walked down to the Mars Pavilion. Some lights were on in there, but the new Pluto Pavilion opposite it was obviously the center of attraction tonight. Though it was late, Bill could see a crowd moving within the glass-walled structure. Probably they were displaying the Plutonians to the press, he thought.

He went around to the staff entrance of the Mars Pavilion and asked for admission. Sid Webster let him in.

"I'm minding the store tonight," Sid said. "Everybody else is across the way."

"How's it been going while I was away?"

"Not bad. Not bad. We had a little breakthrough in linguistics, and Dr. Chiang thinks he's found out something about the oxygen-producing effect."

"A pretty good month," Bill said. He looked at the

screens, which showed the slender forms of Moe and Joe and the other Old Martians in the dwelling chamber upstairs. Idly he walked around the laboratory room, letting his hands rest on this piece of equipment and that. Sid Webster watched him curiously.

"What do you think about those Plutonians?" he asked Bill after a while. "Do they follow the ideas you expressed in your paper?"

"I don't know," Bill said. "It all remains to be seen. We didn't have research facilities on the ship."

"There'll be plenty of excitement ahead, though. With one stroke you've doubled the scope of xenobiology."

Bill smiled. That sounded terribly impressive, somehow. Yet all he had done was take a long journey and scoop some crablike things into a tank of liquid methane. The real work was just beginning.

And there was Neptune, and Jupiter, and Uranus, and Saturn, and all the many moons, and maybe someday the stars—

Work to do tomorrow. And the day after tomorrow, and all the tomorrows after that.

He said, "Why don't you go across and see what's going on over there, Sid?"

"It's my turn to monitor the dials."

"I can do that for you."

"But it's the grand opening of the Pluto Pavilion," Webster protested. "If anybody ought to be there, you're the one!"

"I've had enough celebrations for a while, thanks. Go on! Scoot! I'll do the monitoring for you!"

Mumbling his thanks, Sid headed for the door. Bill slouched down in front of the dials that announced the condition of the environment in the Old Martians' dwelling chamber. Not very exciting work, he thought. But important. It was time to pull back from the excitements, the press conferences, the publicity, and regain his perspective on things.

He stared at the array of monitoring devices. In their glossy surfaces he saw strange reflections: Roger Fancourt, gravely questioning him about Pluto, and Emily laughing as she led him through the walls of the Fair Satellite, and purple crablike creatures slowly moving on a frosty beach. He closed his eyes a moment, and when he opened them the phantoms were gone, and only the prosaic meters and dials remained.